The renegade jabbed the furious Colonel with his gun muzzle. "It's you or me!"

The words were barely out when Flint closed in and swooped down on his prey. One iron fist struck the gunman on the side of his neck; the other hand simultaneously knocked the dragoon Colt away from the Colonel's back. The gun exploded and the slug ploughed into the boards of the porch. The renegade crashed down sidewise, tripping over an artfully placed boot.

He writhed over on his back, snarling.

The gun crashed again.

"Flint! *Be careful*," came Libby's horrified cry through the heavy silence. . . .

RIMROCK RIDERS
was originally published by Jefferson House, Inc.

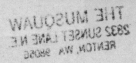
Books by Peter Field

Are there paperbound books you want but cannot find in your retail stores?

You can get any title in print in **POCKET BOOK** editions. Simply send retail price, local sales tax, if any, plus 25¢ (50¢ if you order two or more books) to cover mailing and handling costs to:

MAIL SERVICE DEPARTMENT
    POCKET BOOKS • A Division of Simon & Schuster, Inc.
    1 West 39th Street • New York, New York 10018

Please send check or money order. We cannot be responsible for cash.   *Catalogue sent free on request.*

Titles in this series are also available at discounts in quantity lots for industrial or sales-promotional use. For details write our Special Projects Agency: The Benjamin Company, Inc., 485 Madison Avenue, New York, New York 10022.

Rimrock Riders

A Powder Valley Western

By Peter Field

PUBLISHED BY POCKET BOOKS NEW YORK

RIMROCK RIDERS

Jefferson House edition published 1961

POCKET BOOK edition published August, 1976

This POCKET BOOK edition includes every word contained in
the original, higher-priced edition. It is printed from brand-
new plates made from completely reset, clear, easy-to-read type.
POCKET BOOK editions are published by
POCKET BOOKS,
a division of Simon & Schuster, Inc.,
A GULF+WESTERN COMPANY
630 Fifth Avenue,
New York, N.Y. 10020.
Trademarks registered in the United States
and other countries.

Rimrock Riders

1

Topping out on the crest of Raton Pass, Sam Sloan drew rein and cast his glance backward over the way they had come. He was a stocky and rotund man, clad in bulging bib-overalls and blue denim shirt, and he looked awkward astride the powerful roan, his short legs jutting outward. His beefy moon face was flushed red above the thick blue-black stubble fringing his jowls, but the jet pupils glinting beneath his floppy hat brim were unconquerably cheerful.

Noting this delay, Sam's lanky partner Ezra turned back briefly. For once their little horse herd, subdued by the long arduous climb up to the pass, offered no difficulty and plodded stolidly on. For a few moments the pair sat their saddles, silently gazing.

New Mexico spread open to their view nearly a thousand feet below them, stretching for a hundred miles and more into the south, a tawny desert studded with lofty, golden buttes and barred by chocolate-hued iron ridges. Here and there a faint tinge of green marked the forests of brush. Towering white galleons of cloud cruised the vast horizon.

Crusty old hardshells though they were, neither was wholly oblivious of the majesty of this far-flung land. Such was his lifelong training, however, that not even now did Sloan wholly ignore their immediate concerns.

"Wonder who that is yonder, Ez." His beady eyes squinted almost shut, Sam pointed out a group of tiny horsemen several miles below them and toiling at a snail's pace up the pass. "Yuh don't reckon they could be trailin' us—?"

"Why should they?" Ezra scoffed. Though he had only

7

one eye, a livid knife-scar angling down across the empty
socket of the other, he seldom missed much. He sat
straightbacked and erect, a battered black flatbrim canted
forward to shade his lantern-jawed face, scanning the
mounted party below with his usual sharpness.

"Don't be borrowin' grief, squirt," he admonished gruffly. "We know we bought these broncs fair and square.
Who'd be interested in 'em besides us? . . . Likely that
bunch don't even know we're ahead of 'em," he pursued
tersely. "Shall we shove along about our business?"

Sam only grunted in reply. But as he turned to thrust
on after the strung-out roans in company with Ezra, he
glanced backward discontentedly from time to time. It
was plain he could not get the horsemen behind them altogether out of his mind.

Up here on the higher level much of the baking desert
heat had been left behind. A cooling breeze rustled the
brush and stunted cedars; the rugged ledges of rock broke
up the direct refraction of the sun's glare. The welcome
change presently stirred the horses to awakening spirit,
and the craggy pair were soon busy keeping them in
order.

There were seventeen heavy, rawboned roans in the
bunch they had bought the day before at Haskins' little
Bar 8, near Fort McDonald on the Escondido Indian Reserve in New Mexico. Partners in the Bar ES horse ranch
up north in Powder Valley, Colorado, they counted confidently on grading up their herd with the sturdy qualities
of this rugged stock. Nothing else would have taken them
so far from home in search of the best obtainable.

An hour later Ezra was on the verge of exasperation, so
hard was the task of keeping these salty broncs bunched
and headed the right way. "Thunderation," he burst out
explosively, wiping the sweat from his bony forehead with
upraised arm. "I'm in favor of tossin' these hammerheads
into a rock pen and grabbin' us a breathin' spell!"

"Unh-uh! We're shovin' straight on, Ez—"

"What for?" Ezra stared at Sam in surprise—noting the
other's absent glance to the rear as he did so. He snorted.

"Good cripes! Yuh ain't still worryin' about them hombres behind us, I hope?"

Sloan's indifference to scathing sarcasm, which at another time would have earned his instant rage, was the measure of his secret concern. "No sir." He shook his head decisively. "They ain't worryin' me a bit—because I don't aim to let 'em."

Ez muttered sourly under his breath, but it was noticeable that he voiced no further argument. Fully capable of dominating his squat companion when he chose, this time he did not attempt it. Twenty minutes later, following Sam's backward glance as they topped a rocky rise, the old rawhide was plainly jolted by what he saw. His jaw dropped.

"Say! They do seem to be followin' us," he barked, his tone hardening.

It was true. Although they had turned off the beaten trail north to Trinidad after leaving the pass behind to strike out across the open hills flanking the Culebra range, they had not so far succeeded in shaking off the mounted men far to their rear. Even as he looked Ezra spied the tiny bobbing figures still forging their way directly with ominous persistence.

"Hang it all! It don't make sense, Sam," he exclaimed resentfully. "Yuh don't reckon them fellers are figurin' to—?" He broke off uneasily, hesitating to complete his thought.

Sloan shrugged, paying him scant attention as he hazed the roans vigorously along. "This is wild, lonely country," he tossed back tersely. "Yuh figurin' to stop and ask them hombres what they're after? Or shall we make tracks?"

Ez allowed his actions to speak for him, throwing himself into the work of hustling the spirited horses into a run. They needed little urging, striking sparks off the rocks with their thudding hoofs. Riding recklessly at either side, the partners contented themselves with making sure that none of their charges broke away. Unobserved in this rough country, and keeping to low ground, they had gained more than a mile by the time they next glimpsed their followers; and they did not slack off.

"Ain't no doubt about it now," rasped Ez as the hot afternoon waned and still the band to the rear continued to keep them in view. "They're floggin' our tracks, sure as God made little apples. And it can't be for no good!"

They found cause now to rejoice in the stamina of this prime horseflesh they sought to protect. Not every man on this or any range was as sturdily mounted. Probably by extracting the last ounce of energy from these roans they could outdistance pursuit altogether. But Sam was not inclined to purchase safety at the expense of his horses.

"Watch for a chance to throw that bunch off the trail, Ez," he directed. "Maybe we can strike through some canyon and push along while one of us stays behind to hold 'em off with a rifle."

It was an old but unfailing ruse, if circumstances were right. Ignoring his partner's bossy tone, Ez set about scanning the rough breaks of the lower end of the Culebras. They had not much time. Already the westering sun was touching the ragged crest. In a matter of minutes it dipped from view. There still remained an hour or less of daylight, which would be plenty if they worked fast. Not long thereafter Ez waved toward a rocky cleft angling up toward the heights.

"Swing 'em that way after we hit the shale slope," he sang out.

The spot did not look promising, but Sam had depended too often on his lanky friend to question his judgment now. Busily they curbed the plunging roans, turning them up-slope. It was no slight task to induce these spirited broncs to take to the tortuous canyon, loving the open as horses did by instinct. Somehow they managed it, crowding the last one through the rocky jaws.

It was narrow and gloomy in the sharply rising canyon. The hoofs of the horses made a great racket, striking the naked rock. But Ez congratulated himself they were leaving little trace of their passing; and here at least little herding of any sort was required.

"Shove along while you can," Sloan called, drawing rein to turn aside in the shelter of riven boulders. "I'll see they don't follow us through here—and I'll catch up when I can."

Waving a gnarled hand, Ezra clattered on. For a time there were only these lonely rocks, echoing to the crack and rumble of traveling horses, which it seemed could be heard for a long distance. The big fellow was pleased finally to note the canyon swinging toward the north. They reached its end among high pine-clad slopes just as twilight fell. Ez kept the broncs moving without haste.

Night was thickening when Sam jogged up on the back trail and calmly rejoined his partner. The big man peered at him sharply. "Did yuh drive them birds off?" he barked. "I didn't hear no firin'—"

Sam waved a hand airily. "Didn't need to," he returned. "I saw 'em comin' and got all set, Ez—and they rode right on by."

"Missed the canyon, eh?" Ez grunted. "Good thing. It's way past our time to haul up, if we don't want these roans ganted for good."

In this broken country it was not hard to find a cup in the hills, affording ample graze and ringed about by rocks, where the little bunch could be held by a single man. Turning them out under the stars, they made a camp of sorts. Ez watched the horses settle down while Sam threw a meal together. At the latter's call the tall man rode up and dismounted, in a grumpy mood.

"How do yuh know that wasn't a blind—them hombres ridin' on past the canyon—and they won't come down on us durin' the night?" he demanded.

Sam dished him up a generous plate. "I don't think so, Ez. I heard 'em talkin'. They was trailin' us all right —or they thought so." His chubby face was sober in the firelight. "Yuh reckon they'll backtrack in the mornin' and pick up our sign?"

Ezra refused to worry. "We'll keep a watch tonight and shove on as soon as it's light. If they grab this bunch at all, we'll make 'em earn it."

He took the first trick, awakening his stout companion sometime after midnight. Sloan took over uncomplainingly, and the small hours dragged by. If the chunky man kept watch alertly, there was nothing to disturb him beyond the occasional stamping of the dozing roans.

The heartening odor of coffee brought him back to camp with the first pale streaks of dawn. Ezra was astir. Gulping a hasty breakfast, they were soon in the saddle. Gray shadows still claimed the looming Culebras when they shoved off, and the chill up here was pronounced.

Their first thought was to water the roans. This was accomplished at a rocky spring. Fortunately for them a load of water slowed down the frisky animals, making them almost sedate. The way led downward across steep pine slopes, and there were hazardous places to negotiate. The time seemed short before the sun broached the eastern rim of the plains and gradually warmed their blood.

For several hours they kept a wary watch to the rear. But there was only the laden pack horse jogging patiently along in their wake. This day they saw no sign of human activity other than their own.

"It don't mean they gave us up," warned Ez as the long hot afternoon dragged on. "We'll shove on down to the Bar ES, and if they show up there we'll know how to handle it."

Working down toward the lower slopes where the going was better, they thrust steadily onward. They had developed a system of pushing the horses briskly for an hour, then allowing them ten minutes to graze and rest. It worked surprisingly well. The partners were notorious for covering more miles in a given time with a bunch of horses than was thought possible, and it was no different now. Familiar landmarks at length told them that with luck they would reach home well before dark.

"We made it again, Ez." Sloan showed his snag teeth in a wolfish grin as the little horse ranch came into view. "It was worth-while too! Give 'em a little rest and feed, and this is a nice bunch of stuff to add to our herd."

Ezra's nod was sage. "We stand to make a few dollars

on our work if everything goes right," he allowed with habitual caution.

Sam was about to make a scoffing response when his gaze abruptly became fixed. For a moment he sat the saddle motionless. "Somebody there at the ranch," he whipped out alertly. "Can't be them buzzards we ducked got here this fast—"

Ez gazed keenly with his single eye. He grunted. "We got company, for a fact. . . . We'll turn this stuff in the pasture and go take a look."

It was far from an easy chore to haze the frisky roans through a gate, unfamiliar as they were with this range. At last it was accomplished. Sobering to sternness, the pair slammed the gate shut and turned automatically toward the house. The Bar ES was only a weathered log cabin standing in the shade of patriarchal cottonwoods. Much had happened there, and for a number of years the crusty partners had known no other home. As he drew near, Sam began to swear softly under his breath.

"Blast it all! It ain't nobody but Stevens," he burst out vigorously.

Ez saw that he was right. The tall, broad-shouldered man waiting under the trees, years younger than either of them and in the vigorous prime of life, was none other than Pat Stevens, owner of the Lazy Mare ranch a few miles north in Powder Valley and a friend of long standing.

"Howdy, boy," called Ez gruffly, a note of relief in his voice.

Stevens raised a hand, turning toward his waiting saddle horse as he did so. He started to swing astride. Ezra watched this with dropped jaw. "Hold on, Stevens! We just got here. Where yuh goin'—?" he began.

Pat gave them both a cool look and shrugged. "Sloan don't think much of my being here," he retorted. "So I'll be going. If I'm 'only Stevens,' you can hardly miss me!"

Swinging down to join the other on the ground, Sam found himself forced to talk fast, telling about their recent adventure to explain his unguarded exclamation. "Dang yuh, yuh knowed there was a reason," he accused, fully aware of the younger man's habit of enjoying his dry joke at their expense.

Pat's gray eyes twinkled quizzically. He was genuinely glad to see them back after their two-week trip. "So you picked up some horseflesh, eh? And tolled a band of horse thieves into the valley after you—"

Sam fired up promptly, till Ez laughed at him. "Let him make his crack, Sam," he advised tolerantly. "We know we didn't do anything of the kind."

"Oh, I don't know." Stevens was gazing absently out across the range. "Here comes a bunch hard after you now. It could be your neighbor Catterson's crew on the way home, of course—but they look like total strangers to me," he observed ironically.

The pair whirled. As Pat said, five mounted men were advancing boldly toward the ranch. Ez looked that way hard. "*Can* that be them hombres?" he breathed tightly. "You saw 'em closer than me, Sam—what about it?"

Sloan hesitated briefly. "Looks like the same crowd from here," he muttered uneasily. "Might be a good idea not to let 'em get too close either!" He started to pull his carbine out of the boot, only to desist as his gaze fixed. His next words were a croak of consternation. "Holy smoke! *They* ain't owlhoots! Take a good look. . . . That hombre in front is sportin' a law badge—"

"Don't be too sure that means anything," Ez whipped out harshly. "Watch this, now, till we see what it amounts to!"

The party of strangers jogged forward in ominous silence. Their leader, apparently a sheriff, waved imperiously toward the pasture. "Who owns them HO8 roans?" he demanded flatly across a space of thirty or forty yards.

Ez pushed forward. "Ain't seen you around since we picked up them horses three days ago. How do yuh know what their brands are, mister?"

Plainly used to authority, the leader showed him a leathery face dark with anger and resolve. "I asked yuh a question," he roared. "Are yuh goin' to answer it? . . . I said who claims them broncs?"

"If you're fixin to dispute it, I reckon we do," drawled Ez, bringing his gun forward. "So what of it, neighbor?"

"Sorry. But they happen to be stolen stock," announced the lawman brusquely, ignoring the threat of Ezra's gun. "My posse'll take charge of 'em right now."

2

"You're a liar," flashed Sam Sloan hotly, his chest swelling like a pouter pigeon's. "Be a little more careful with your talk, stranger!"

The possemen, moving about indolently as they looked the place over, suddenly froze to immobility at these words. Their stern-faced leader scowled down at Sloan heavily. He had a good command of his temper.

"Yuh mean I'm not takin' them broncs in charge—is that it, friend?" he grated carefully.

"I mean they're not stolen! And I can prove it," declared Sam as vigorously as before. Fumbling in a shirt pocket, he brought out a much-folded paper. "Here's the bill of sale, coverin' their number, points and brands—and signed by old Joe Haskins down there in New Mexico, all legal and proper!"

The sheriff waved it away, not even offering to examine it. "Don't mean a thing," he insisted dourly. "I know. The fact is, those roans are U. S. Government property, mister—stolen straight from Fort McDonald Army post. . . . Didn't yuh take a close look at that HO8 road brand?" he drove on scathingly. "A fool could see it's been over-branded, with the U. S. made into an O8, and the H added!"

The cold logic of this claim, whatever its accuracy, had never occurred to them before and was like a dash of cold water to the grizzled partners. They exchanged a lightning glance. "And just who would you be, while we're on the subject?" rumbled Ezra suspiciously.

"Lybolt's the name," murmured the lawman smoothly. "Funny yuh ain't heard of me this close to New Mexico!"

"Well, we ain't," retorted Sam defiantly, not at all intimidated by the glowering members of the posse. "If you're what you claim to be, how come there's no Army man in this bunch?" he probed shrewdly.

The members of the posse looked quickly at each other. "Oh, hell. Why argue with him, Gif?" one snorted. "Say the word and we'll pick up them horses and be on our way!"

Lybolt lifted a staying hand, exhibiting a phlegmatic patience. "No, hold on. The Army *is* on the hunt. It just happens I followed a hunch of my own—and it turned out to be the right one."

"There's a lot of 'just happen' in your talk, neighbor," fired out Ez testily. "We got t' be sure. What about this bill of sale we got, fair and square. We paid for them roans! Are yuh seein' to it that we get our money back?"

Pat had not offered to take part in the altercation at any time, nor did he have any comment to make now. But Gif Lybolt's delay interested him much.

"There's a sayin' down our way, let the buyer beware," the sheriff said finally. "You two're certainly not goin' out of your way to cooperate with me. That bill is faked anyway. It has to be. Old Haskins is sure to disown it—"

"Let's get this straight," interposed Sam flatly. "Just what *do* yuh figure we owe you, Lybolt—now or later?"

"Yuh sure shook me off your trail the hard way," the other flung back hardily. "If yuh was in the clear, what would it cost yuh to stop and talk when yuh first seen us, instead of forcin' us to ride way up here to hell and gone?"

His slighting reference to Powder Valley gained him no favor whatever. "It would've cost us those horses, no matter what. And well you know it!" rasped Ezra angrily. "If you're so sure of us, why don't yuh take us in custody, Mister Sheriff?" He emphasized the title sardonically, his lanky frame strung taut as a bowstring. "Just try it, is all!"

Either he had forced Lybolt into a corner, or the man's patience was wearing thin. He leveled a gnarled finger at Ezra threateningly.

"Don't give me any orders, old terrapin. Just stay right where yuh are, the lot of yuh. . . . The real crook's down below the line in New Mexico, if yuh got to know, and I aim to deal with him in my own way—at my convenience. Right now," Lybolt proceeded tonelessly, "I expect my boys to pick up those broncs—and if yuh try to interfere yuh can take the consequences. That's a declaration of intentions!"

Sam and Ez looked at each other again uneasily as the posse moved slowly toward the pasture. They did not offer any vehement protest, although Sloan continued to grumble sourly. Even now they might have taken decisive action but for one thing. The fact that the roans were said to have been stolen from the U. S. Army—which might, for all they knew, be the case—served as an effective check.

Still Stevens held his peace; and if he continued to gaze at Gif Lybolt in an embarrassingly candid manner, his disinterested demeanor called for no overt objection. It was impossible to judge whether the self-styled sheriff felt uneasy or not. But when he noted that the disputed roans were being swiftly rounded up and turned toward the pasture gate he started to turn away with something suspiciously like relief.

"Remember now," he called back the warning. "This is the law. Give me trouble in any manner, shape or form, and it'll go harder with yuh!" With this parting shot he jogged out of hearing.

Having secured the last of the frisky roans, the posse was rapidly hazing the stuff once more onto open range. With a triumphant air the men headed them south and shoved them rapidly along, as if anxious to get well out of sight before darkness closed down.

Ez and Sam watched the departure of the horses in

open dismay. "Holy mackerel! *That* was short and sweet,"
breathed Sam anxiously. "What do we do now, Stevens?"

Pat was privately amused at their instinctive reliance
on his judgment. "I can only tell you what I'd do in your
case," he countered easily. He broke off there, sobering.
"Just how sure are you that this Lybolt is what he claims
to be, and not the leader of a bunch of smooth phonies?"

"We ain't," returned Ez dourly. "We landed down there
near Fort McDonald, spotted them roans on Haskins'
Bar 8, made our dicker and drove 'em away. Didn't have
no contact with local authorities at all. . . . But Lybolt
did follow us up here from Raton Pass—we know that."

Stevens thought it over unhurriedly. "You were here
on your own range, with a bill of sale in your pocket," he
proceeded mildly. "I'd have backed you up if you
decided to chase that crowd off the place in a hurry—"

"Don't get us wrong!" Sam spoke up quickly. "We
ain't backin' down to nobody, boy. Yuh heard Lybolt
yourself. If that is Army horseflesh and we got tough
about it, we'd land in the soup. And don't try to tell us
different!"

Pat nodded. He did not really question their courage,
knowing the doughty pair of old. "So that's the rub."
He began to laugh. "Leave it to you two to get stuck
with stolen Army horses! This Haskins you speak of
must've talked like a Dutch uncle. . . . What'll you be
doing next?"

"Wasn't that way, Stevens," Ez said tersely. "I reckon
we did most of the talkin' ourselves. No use lyin'. But
Haskins showed us his own bill of sale, and he seemed
happy enough with it. *I* never questioned it was good."

Pat's smile was tight. "Maybe you should've," he suggested.

For once they appeared crushed, unable to find a
further word to say in their own defense. More than once
they had caught Pat in a similar position and had exhibited
scant mercy. For a moment he relished their chagrin,
smiling on them benignly. Then the smile faded.

"Well," his tone turned practical, "leaving the rest

of this deal aside, in your boots I'd certainly be interested in knowing where these broncs go from here."

It was a new idea to them, and it made sense. Both partners perked up hopefully. Yet Ez remained unconquerably suspicious. "Why do yuh say that?" he demanded.

Stevens shrugged. "I could be wrong. But usually when the law overtakes stolen stock in the possession of a couple of pecky hombres like you two, there's an arrest made on the spot. It seemed to me this Lybolt was interested mainly in grabbing those broncs—and got away with it."

From the first the pair had fully expected to fight off an attempt to take them in custody. The omission now seemed fraught with a double significance. It threw a new light on the situation, and one which aroused the crusty partners to fresh anger. "By grab, there's that against him! . . . Come on, Stevens!" Sam was all for instant action, wheeling toward the horses. "We'll tag along at the tail end of this parade. And Lybolt better turn up in the right place with them AWOL roans, or he'll be hearin' from us!"

Pat stood unmoving. "Hold on, Sam." He shook his head, smiling regretfully. "I figured you'd be home yesterday or today, and rode over to say howdy. I didn't come prepared to start off on a week's vacation, even for such a cause."

Sloan halted beside his bronc and looked at Pat across its back, frowning. "What—?" If he was trying to sound incredulous, he certainly succeeded. "Yuh ain't lettin' your old friends down now, are yuh?"

"Never mind the soft soap," Stevens said dryly. "I don't find myself obliged to ride off Lord knows where because you two pulled a boner! You can get that idea out of your head fast."

This trio had never pulled any punches in dealing with one another. It was one of the proofs of their deep, if inarticulate, attachment. Moreover, it usually seemed to work out to a mutual advantage in the end.

"Wait just a minute, boy." Though normally the most

peppery of the partners, Ezra could on occasion assume an unexpected dignity. It was one of the secrets of his strong hold on Pat's regard. "Sam is talkin' a little fast maybe. But this is no time for foolin'. Don't yuh get it? Them roans mean a lot to us, and we're askin' yuh for help now, when we need it."

This modest approach caught Stevens off guard, as Ezra hoped. The younger man delayed briefly, while the two old rawhides watched him and waited. "That's putting it a little different, anyhow," grumbled Pat finally. "You must know work is always waiting for me over there on the Lazy Mare. . . . Hang it all, why did I ever go to the trouble of adopting you two anyway?"

Sam's relieved grin flashed out and he endeavored to conceal it. "It ain't as though we never helped yuh get some of that work done," he reminded shrewdly.

Pat's nod of assent was tempered with a grunt. They could see he was making up his mind slowly.

"You're asking for help. If I come along on this fool's errand I don't want to hear a squawk the first time I try to use my head—"

"Not at all, not at all," returned Sam quickly. "When did we ever contradict yuh, Stevens—seriously I mean?" He had the grace to show brief confusion as Ezra glared at him accusingly. "Well, once in a while, maybe, just to keep things lively," he said, grinning brazenly.

Pat shrugged, hitching his pants up at the waist. "So that's settled—I hope." His pause was slight. "So don't start making a fuss the minute I open my mouth, will you? I'll have to make a quick trip home first, before we take off—"

Sam showed instant consternation. "What in time do yuh have to do that for?" he complained loudly. "Dang it, Stevens! If those birds are horse thieves after all, they'll be sure to lose us! Can't yuh see we ain't got an hour to waste?"

Pat looked at him austerely. "I was about to say you've got two choices. You can either wait here for me —or you can shove off and I'll catch up when I get around to it. Suit yourself."

"We'll wait." Ezra made the decision hastily, before Sam found further objections to voice. "We only just got home after a hard trip. Make it snappy, boy, and meanwhile we'll eat a square meal and do a few chores. Sam may want to shave—"

"Go shave your grandmother!" burst out Sam disgustedly. "You'll have time before we get started. If we ever do!"

He had no more to say as Stevens swung astride without ado and struck out for the Lazy Mare. But he peered after the younger man sharply, plainly hoping his pointed remarks would urge the other to all possible speed.

Disappointment over their disastrous luck held the partners silent as they prepared supper and ate. As long as the evening light lasted, Sam repeatedly glanced over the trail to town, although it was impossible that Pat should reappear for several hours at least. Darkness fell and the little man resigned himself to wait, chafing and fuming inwardly.

"Why don't yuh go to bed?" roared Ez finally in exasperation. "Or are yuh figurin' to stay up all night—"

Usually the more placid of the two, tonight Sam was inconsolable. "We were fools to wait," he stormed. "We shook them hombres off our own trail without any great trouble—and they'll do the same to us! . . . Dang us for a couple of lamebrains, Ez. I don't believe that Lybolt was a sheriff at all!"

"Why didn't you blast his head off, then?" snarled Ez. "It's you that keeps on cryin' about the Army—"

"If I did that and it turned out he *was* a sheriff . . ." began Sam.

Ez threw a boot at him savagely. Sam ducked it and whirled to face his attacker, his face black as a thundercloud. There were the makings of a fine quarrel here; but before it got started hoofs thudded outside in the yard, and a moment later Stevens stuck his head in the door.

"Did I hear shooting?" he inquired with mock concern.

They were so glad to see him that both turned to him at once, their own differences forgotten. "Yuh didn't let no grass grow under yuh, boy," averred Sam approvingly, all his former objections now forgotten. "Shall we saddle up right off?"

Pat looked surprised, but only shrugged. "Kind of late, isn't it? But whatever you say——"

"Go to bed, the two of you," Ez bellowed, his shirt halfway off. "My nerves are clean frazzled with foolishness. I'm gettin' my rest and takin' off at first light in the mornin'. You can do as you're a mind to!"

Strangely enough it was Sam who objected loudly to being roused out of bed at three o'clock the following morning. Ez would listen to nothing as he tossed a hurried breakfast on the lantern-lit table and urged the others to action.

"We can't see no tracks this early, yuh old fool," protested Sloan disgustedly.

"Don't need to. We can be overtakin' them buzzards while they sleep. Time enough to pick up their tracks later on."

Packs had been thrown together the night before, and they soon got up fresh mounts. It was still pitch-dark when the three turned their backs on the Bar ES, shoving off toward the south.

They traveled steadily. Pale dawn streaked the east at last, and presently the ghostly bulk of the high Culebras loomed on their right. It was half an hour before they could make out the ground underfoot with any clearness. Ezra, for years a noted tracker, began to cast about busily for sign of the confiscated horses.

It was a long time before he spotted what seemed a smudged print or two heading in the right direction. "Ground's too rocky here," he commented briefly. "We'll pick up a clear track farther on——"

They thrust on as the sun leaped above the flat horizon, hung low for what seemed a long time and then began to climb. Stevens for one paid no marked attention to the ground they were covering, content to make steady progress. But Sam showed an increase of uneasiness at their continued failure to pick up the trail they hoped to follow, grumbling under his breath.

"You and your early start!" he shouted at Ezra, unable

longer to contain his mounting irritation. "We'll be lucky if your blasted foolishness don't set us back a day. Is that what I worked so hard persuadin' Stevens to come along for?"

Ez failed to take fire as promptly as he usually did. He found it difficult to conceal his own concern at the moment. Still he had an answer.

"Said we'd pick them birds up later, didn't I?" He pointed ahead toward a narrow gap between flat-topped buttes. "If I ain't crazy they *had* to go through there—and that's where we'll pick 'em up. You'll see if I ain't right."

Sam subsided, but only long enough to cover the three or four miles to the gap. Once there they examined the narrow passage from wall to wall but found no sign whatever of the passing of horses. The nearest approach to life was a lone deer trail in the dust, and the pad-marks left by prowling coyotes. Ezra stared about briefly in disbelief.

"Dang it all," he exploded harshly. "Does that Lybolt think he's makin' fools of us, or what?" His tone was one of fierce resentment at this unmerited betrayal.

It was plain enough to all that he had miscalculated badly and there was not even the slightest indication of the direction in which the confiscated horses had been driven.

3

SAM WHIRLED on Pat with flashing eyes. "There yuh are, Stevens! All the proof yuh need that Lybolt is nothing but a horse thief. And yuh just stood there and let him put the snatch on our roans without liftin' a finger!"

Pat cocked a brow at him, unmoved. "That so?" He sounded faintly surprised at this announcement. "So what do you expect me to do now?"

"Nothin' for us to do but turn around and go back

home," Sam ranted. "Unless Ez thinks he can pick up their trail somewhere in the hills. Probably they didn't come this way at all!"

"Take it easy now. Things may not be as bad as all that." Pat displayed bored patience. "For my part, I move we shove along south—"

"What for?"

"We're bound to pick those hombres up before we strike Raton Pass. They came from down this way—and they'll go back."

Insulted by any suggestion opposed to his own, Sam appealed vehemently to Ezra. The tall tracker looked about him absently and shrugged. "Nothin' to lose by shovin' on a ways," he said finally. "It's either that or forget the whole thing."

They shoved on to the tune of Sam's doleful complaints. Midday came and passed. Although Ezra studied their surroundings keenly, he did not at any time turn far out of the straight trail. The afternoon waned, and it grew late without their discovering any sign of the elusive trail they sought.

"What makes yuh so sure they come this way?" demanded Sam. "That could be just what they want us to think!"

"Oh, I don't know." The Lazy Mare owner was tantalizingly calm. "Lybolt must've had a pretty good idea that somebody would follow him. I wouldn't put it past him to give you a hard time after the trick you played on him."

Ez looked up quickly, then nodded. "Yuh got somethin' there, boy." He sounded hopeful. "We can shove along an extra hour or two tonight, with no trail to lose anyway. Tomorrow I'll make a real stab at pickin' up the sign of those roans."

They rode till well after dark, then turned into the hills to follow a creek. Here they found graze for the horses and wood for a fire. There was some forced good humor as they ate supper, but it was not overly successful. Sam was inclined toward gloomy discouragement, sure by now that they had lost the money paid for the horses. Certainly their poor luck today did not augur well for the morrow.

They turned in and in a matter of minutes all were breathing regularly. Even the yelp of coyotes in the higher hills did not disturb their rest. Once more Ez was the first astir next morning, and as before he drove them to action. Light was just breaking through the hills by the time they shoved off.

Instead of returning at once to the open sagebrush plain a few hundred feet below, today they clung to the hills. Sloan thought this a needless hardship, and he found plenty of remarks to make. The others were just about fed up with his grousing when, at one point, Ezra found horse sign. Although the ground here was too flinty to tell much, he persisted. Twenty minutes later he pointed out the tracks of a band of horses which had passed by within the last day or so.

"Think that was Lybolt, do yuh?" Sam scoffed. "Why, there could even be a few wild broomtails in these hills—"

Pat shook his head, smiling faintly. "No sale, Sam. Since when have you seen the wild ones running around shod?"

Sam's eyes widened. He took a fresh gander at the tracks and grunted. "Well, maybe they are wearin' shoes. Some trail herd, runnin' its remuda up here for grass, like as not!" He could not be persuaded that their luck had turned at last.

Pat laughed at him. "Of course if you don't *want* to locate those roans you bought," he jibed, "we needn't hunt any longer."

Sam was not to be cozened. "We can shove on a ways farther and see," he allowed grudgingly.

Even now it was not easy to pursue the trail of the horses with any speed. As Pat suggested, if this was indeed the little herd they sought, the men in charge were consistently doing their best to hide the evidence of their passing. For an hour Ez worked doggedly, unravelling the faint sign, till they got out of the hardpan country. After that it was easier.

Lybolt's men must have thought they had thrown off

pursuit at last, for the way now led downward toward open range. Not till the hills around Raton Pass began to appear on the horizon did the trio come out on a high spot from which a view could be obtained. Despite the handicap to his sight, Ez seldom missed much. He drew up in waist-high brush and pointed mutely beyond. Several miles ahead and far down the tumbled slope they made out a moving bunch of horses and the tiny figures of Lybolt's posse, steadily hazing them on.

"By gravy, it's them!" Sam sucked in his breath sharply. "We can overhaul them hombres in a couple of hours if we fly at it—"

Pat promptly shook a decided negative. "Nothing like that, Sam." His tone was measured. "You had your chance to dicker with Lybolt there on the Bar ES. What else would you say now?"

Sam looked crestfallen. "Yuh mean we got to watch 'em drive our horses right on?" he blurted out in dismay. "Then what're we doin' here now?"

"I *thought* we aimed to make sure those roans got back to the Army post where Lybolt claims they belong," retorted Stevens tartly. "If you can think of a better way to check on him, come out with it."

Sam subsided and Ez nodded sagely. "Stevens is right. We don't even want that crowd to know we're followin' 'em," he seconded stoutly. "We'll tag along at a safe distance and watch what goes on."

They waited for some minutes until the drovers faded from sight beyond the next rise, then thrust on. With their objective no longer in doubt they made good time. When next they glimpsed the traveling roans, they were considerably closer. Pat noted that if Lybolt's men had any further thought of the back trail, they no longer bothered to look behind.

Watching them file from sight in the rocks near the pass, Sam was struck by a new idea. "When they start goin' down the pass, that trail'll be in sight for a long time, Stevens," he pointed out uneasily. "They're bound to spot us trailin' after 'em!"

Pat had been weighing this. "Raton is the easiest way

down," he gave back. "It's not the only way. If we can locate a canyon running down to the south from the rim, we can hit bottom at pretty nearly the same time they do."

They swung off the trail and made for another part of the rim. The first canyon they struck was narrow and precipitous. Ez shook his head dourly. "That's a drop-off," he averred. "We got to hunt farther—"

Ten minutes later they struck a winding defile which led downward. It appeared to offer a clear, if difficult, passage. Forcing their way in at the top, they were soon dropping rapidly, the weathered crags of the cliffs looming overhead. At one point they came to a sheer slant where it was necessary for the horses to slide precariously downward on bunched hoofs; but that was the worst. The lower canyon was choked with piñon and had to be negotiated with care. Half an hour later the close walls drew back and they glimpsed the rolling sage spread of the New Mexican plain opening out.

Reaching the rocky canyon's mouth, they looked guardedly in the direction of the pass trail. It could be seen here and there, angling downward at a more leisurely slant. But it was some time before they spotted Lybolt's party not far from the bottom.

They set off that way. Just here the hills were too rough to allow them to keep the quarry in clear sight for longer than a few minutes at a time. "We can draw up on 'em some, long as we keep to the brush," Ez opined.

Clinging to the hollows and maintaining a narrow watch ahead, they were about to round the end of a short ridge when Sloan, who was in the lead, suddenly reined back hastily, waving an urgent warning to the others. At the moment they heard the dull tattoo of rapidly approaching hoofs. If Lybolt's entire posse was coming their way there would be no time to hide.

While they sat frozen in the saddle, uncertain of what to expect, a single roan horse pounded into view. Wholly unaccompanied and without a saddle, it snorted at sight of them and started to wheel away.

"Hey! That's a stray from Lybolt's bunch," exclaimed Sam tightly.

Taking in the situation at a glance, Stevens thought fast. He whipped his coiled lariat off the saddle horn and built a loop as he started forward. The roan had not taken half-a-dozen buck jumps before the rope settled snugly over its neck. Pat snubbed it down and turned back.

Ez sat his saddle looking the prize over dubiously. "Wonder how it got away from that bunch?" he voiced his doubt, glancing across at the others.

Pat couldn't say. "Ten to one somebody'll come looking for it directly," he guessed. "We'll just take it along with us and keep out of sight."

Sam was not averse to such a course. The roan was a valuable animal, white-stockinged with its proud head held high. "Lybolt won't get this one again as easy as he did the first time," he declared as he looked it over. "I reckon yuh see now why we bought that bunch, Stevens."

Pat nodded his assent. "Shall we move on?" he suggested, looking about alertly.

Turning back now, they swung wide to avoid discovery. Ezra kept a wary watch to the rear, and after climbing a rise he reported that Lybolt's crew seemed to be shoving steadily on as before. Pat weighed the intelligence.

"How far is it to Fort McDonald, would you say?" he queried.

Sam thought it was eighteen or twenty miles west. "They can make it tonight by pluggin'," he added.

It suited Stevens. "We'll see what they do."

The better part of an hour later Sloan climbed the shoulder of a butte to gaze beyond. He turned back hastily to join the others in some bewilderment. "They're two or three miles ahead and pushin' right along," he reported. "And Stevens—down in the hollow yonder there's another stray grazin'!"

"What?" For a moment Stevens did not take it in completely. "Not *another* one, Sam—?"

The stocky man nodded vigorously. "That's what I saw." He broke off, a shrewd look coming over his face. "Yuh don't reckon this could be some kind of bait—?"

"Somethin' crooked is goin' on, that's for sure," interposed Ez gruffly. "They might just possibly overlook one stray, thinkin' themselves plenty safe down here on their home grounds. But two——?" His tone said he would never believe it.

Turning the led roan over to Sam, Pat rode up for his own look. He took his time gazing over the range. When he came back his mind was made up.

"Take Ez's rope and come with me, Sam," he called out briskly. "We'll close in on that bronc and pick it up. I don't savvy exactly what this is about," he added, "but we're about to find out!"

Sam quickly complied. Separating and riding down into the hollow, the two soon cornered the stray and put a line on it. Once its capture was effected, Sam gazed about them apprehensively. But the vast New Mexican afternoon remained peaceful. No one rode out of the brush suddenly to inquire what they were doing.

Ez joined them, shaking his head. "That's two," he said, scanning the second horse with undisguised approval. "Not much doubt there's something phony afoot here——"

"Could be. We've lost sight of Lybolt's crowd about as long as I want to," said Pat. "We'll shove on ahead, Ez, and Sam can follow with the horses."

Ez was ready, although Sloan protested somewhat grumpily. With Pat in the lead the pair rode on at an amended pace. Twenty minutes later they spotted the lawman's posse, jogging along as calmly as if nothing had happened. The roans were stretched out in a loose string, with the possemen scattered along either side. Ez waggled his grizzled head.

"One of them boys is pullin' a fast one," he declared. "Yuh don't count a small bunch of that size every fifteen minutes—but somebody has to know them strays are droppin' out, especially in this open country."

"Horses wouldn't stray far here," Pat nodded agreement. "The plateau would cut them off from the north. And a few miles south the range peters out into open desert. . . . It could be that somebody intends to pick these horses up later!"

"They'll be huntin' some, if they don't see our sign and figure some Indians beat 'em to it," Ez returned.

They were even more certain that some crooked scheme was going on when they came upon a third stray. Like the first, this one took them by complete surprise and they were long in capturing it. Yet they had time. Even now no posseman came jogging back to round up the truant. They had no choice but to conclude it was by deliberate design.

Sam grinned broadly when he saw them coming back with the horse. "Keep this up long enough and we'll have our bunch back," he crowed.

Pat was less inclined to treat it as a joke. "This settled one thing in my mind," he said soberly. "Lybolt would be sure to miss three horses out of seventeen, if he didn't know the answer. I'm for tagging him close from here on out, boys. But we can't drag these strays all over New Mexico."

Sam turned to point back toward the hills. "I saw what looked like an abandoned ranch off yonder," he announced. "There must be an old work corral around somewheres we could turn 'em into."

It was a possibility. Swinging that way purposefully, they succeeded in locating a tumble-down ranch cabin with a pole corral in its rear. It was the work of ten minutes to make it stout enough to hold the roans.

"Shall we shove the pack horse in there with 'em?" Sam inquired.

Pat's hesitation was brief. "No—bring it along. Don't forget we're going to be away from here for a while," he reminded. "Finding our pack horse with those strays— if anyone should—would be a dead giveaway."

"That's right too." Sloan looked guilty. "Come on, then. Crowd the roans in there and we'll shove off."

They lost no time turning the strays into the pen and barring it shut. "I want to draw right up on Lybolt if we can," Pat announced. "It'll soon be getting dark. It would be easy to lose him close to Fort McDonald like this. And it might be our biggest mistake."

They set off quickly, but it seemed a long time before

they spotted any sign of life on the rolling plain. The forage grass thinned out and greasewood took its place. Fortunately for them, as the setting sun sent its slanting rays across the barren wasteland it picked out the glossy coats of the band of roans at a considerable distance. Pat pointed them out, a thin haze of golden dust marking their position. Later they began to draw up on the quarry just as the squat buildings of a desert country village showed far off over the swells.

"Must be Fort McDonald yonder," Pat remarked.

Sam promptly corrected him. "That's the Escondido Agency, Stevens. The fort is two or three miles beyond," he said. "This must be Sheriff Lybolt's bailiwick, I expect—a few supply stores and a saloon or two, besides the Agency. Haskins told us about it."

Circling, they hurried on till the little settlement was between them and the posse. In the evening light they felt safe in closing in boldly, and were in time to see the roans driven in at the upper end of the single street.

"Look at that, now." Sam pointed. "It looks like they're drivin' that stock in some private corral, don't it?"

It was true. Lybolt's men were hazing the horses briskly into an enclosure with a high board fence. It was next to what looked like a supply warehouse, and certainly it was no part of an Army installation.

"Somethin' queer goin' on right there," Ez averred. "Unless Lybolt is holdin' them HO8 critters till he notifies the Army brass." He turned toward Stevens. "What do yuh suggest now, boy?"

"I'm riding on in for a look at this so-called town," returned Pat easily. "Never can tell what you may learn from a look around—"

"What if Lybolt spots us?" asked Sam.

"What if he does?" Pat echoed lightly. "We've certainly a right to be down here. He had his chance to pinch you two, and he didn't want it. . . . Shall we go?"

Without further ado they rode forward through thickening evening shadows to enter the adobe-walled street of the little desert town.

4

Fort McDonald Village, standing in one corner of the Indian reservation a couple of miles from the Army post, appeared to be small but lively. Range men were moving about or talking in groups on the supply store porch. The trio saw blanketed Navajos standing here and there, stolid as statues or moving about without haste. There were two saloons, before one of which—the Hitch Rail—a bunch of off-duty cavalrymen were skylarking. Ezra ran his eye over the score or so of buildings and moved toward the second saloon.

"Where yuh headin' now?" Sam rasped.

"We'll get a little somethin' to cut the dust," was the terse answer.

"Good idea." Pat nodded. "We'll side you there, Ez."

They had their drink, glancing about them with unobtrusive curiosity. Pat noted a freighter or two in the place, and a grizzled old-timer who may have been an Army guide. No one paid them any particular heed, an indication that strangers in Fort McDonald were nothing unusual.

When they had finished Pat tossed a coin on the bar and turned away. In front of the place the three halted. The supply store diagonally across the wide street was the biggest place in town. Apparently it was also the busiest. A weathered sign, T. GUNDEL, ran across the top of the porch.

Stevens was taking note of this when Sam urgently nudged him with an elbow. "There's Lybolt now," the stocky man muttered, keeping his voice down. "He's talkin' to a couple men there on the store porch."

He was right. The low, arcaded porch of the huge establishment ran the full length of the building, with several entrances strung along at intervals. Near one of these doors the lawman stood in confidential talk with two other men. Dusk was gradually thickening, but Pat was still able to make out the Army uniform worn by one of them who looked like a captain or major. The other, obviously a business man, wore an open vest over a white shirt, and his face under the fancy white Stetson was round and hard. Pat sized him up as probably the Indian agent—something in his slightly pompous bearing marked him as being of considerable importance here.

"Hobnobbin' real cosy, ain't they?" Ez commented, his single eye slitted almost shut.

Sam grunted agreement. "Wonder if Lybolt is tellin' that officer about the roans," he murmured.

"Their talk would probably interest us at that," Pat allowed lazily. "I'd sure like to overhear Lybolt's explanation of those three missing strays!"

Although a local sheriff would ostensibly work in unison with Army forces, Pat knew that a certain amount of jealousy usually existed. The Government generally paid for such cooperation as it received from the hardy civilians, who were apt to look on Army personnel as officious interlopers.

"I expect we could find out at the fort fast enough whether those roans were stolen Army stock or not," hazarded Sam, gazing across steadily at the officer.

"Not much question about it," Pat said. "Still—it is queer that Lybolt didn't turn the broncs over to them right away."

Ez was framing a comment, glancing about warily to make sure he was not overheard. He never got his chance to speak, however. A man stepped out of the saloon behind them, pausing to look at them hard.

"What are you duffers after here?" he grated in a challenging tone.

Looking at him carefully, Pat recognized one of Lybolt's possemen who had driven the horses back from Powder Valley. His iron face was almost square, and a slight cast in one eye gave him a sinister aspect.

"You should know," Pat said quickly before the peppery

partners had time to pop off. "To be frank, neighbor, my
friends are worried about the money they paid for those
roans you took away from them. Anything wrong with
that?"

The man snorted. As tall as Pat, and fully fifty or sixty
pounds heavier, he did not lack for authority of either
voice or manner. "Go after old Joe Haskins," he advised
roughly. "It ain't overly healthy for yuh on this range.
Do I make myself clear?"

"If yuh mean can we savvy a bluff when we run into
one, the answer is yes," began Ez truculently. He started
to shove close, by no means intimidated.

"All right—never mind. Just skip it," Pat interposed
hastily, cutting the one-eyed man off and stopping him
in his tracks.

"Don't know whether I will or not." Ez had his dander
up. "Whoever this tough baby is, maybe he'll explain why
it ain't healthy for law-abidin' citizens on Government
land—" He glowered savagely at the posseman, disinclined
to make any concessions whatever.

"Blow away, old man," the burly fellow growled.
"After yuh get all done just move along, and the chances
are yuh won't get hurt."

He sounded so sure of himself that Pat nudged Ezra
to restrain him from further baiting. "What he says makes
sense, Ez," he broke in curtly. "Haskins was the one who
took your money for horses he claimed he had the right
to sell. We can ask him for an explanation. From his
answer we'll know where we stand."

"You're usin' your savvy now," the posseman rasped.
"Why don't yuh just do that—and the sooner the better."

Pat turned away, urging his ruffled companions toward
the horses. "Cut out the growling," he continued as they
moved up the street. "We're spotted now—and we don't
want to spoil what little chance we do have of learning
anything at all."

"You mean you're takin' that hombre's orders to get
out of town?" grumbled Sam disgustedly. "It don't sound
like you at all, Stevens!"

"No harm in letting that bird think we're pulling out,

anyhow," returned Pat levelly. "Then maybe he'll forget about us."

"Oh, I get it." As they reached the horses Sam glanced at the younger man carefully. "Just what do yuh think he's tryin' to keep us from seein', boy?"

Pat shrugged. "Who knows?" A backward look told him the man was still watching them narrowly from the saloon. "Let him think we're gone, and there's a good chance we may find out faster. . . . I've got a hunch," he continued as they turned down the street, "that whatever it is, it concerns those roans—"

They rode out of town, discussing the situation in guarded words. Dusk had thickened rapidly in the past few minutes, a gray shade obscuring the open range. In a matter of rods they made sure of no longer being seen; but Pat insisted on circling town some distance away before they ventured to turn back.

Since the village was planted squarely within the Indian reservation and there were no private land holdings to bother about, they encountered no fences. "What *are* we figurin' to do now?" Ez queried.

"For one thing, I want to know if those roans are staying in that yard," was Pat's answer. "We saw Lybolt talking to an officer. If he reported their recovery, probably a detail would be after the stock in short order. If it's still there it could mean it wasn't reported." Pat was studying the shadowy outlines of buildings on the edge of town. "We'll leave our ponies in back of a shed where we can find them, and shove up closer on foot."

They dismounted finally, ground-anchored their mounts and set off quietly toward the high-fenced wagon yard into which they had watched the HO8 horses being turned. It was dark now, and although people were moving about they reached the corner of the board fence without being detected.

"Too high to see over," growled Ez, examining the barrier briefly.

"Get hold of my boot," Pat directed. "I'll step up—"

Sam made a stirrup of his hands and the younger man eased himself up. His head came above the top of the boards, but the gloom was so thick that he could make out little. He heard horses stirring uneasily in the enclosure, and remained for some seconds straining his senses.

"Shake it up, can't yuh?" Sloan puffed, staggering under his rugged weight. "You're cuttin' my hands in two!"

Pat lowered himself and straightened up. "The roans are there," he affirmed. "I can't see them. But there's no doubt about it. Lybolt hasn't turned that stock over to the Army yet—"

"Are yuh sayin' he's a crook?" Sam queried flatly.

"Not that, exactly." Stevens hesitated. "But we've felt all along that there's something phony about this whole deal. This just about clinches it."

"So do we go straight to the Army post and find out what the score is, or what?" demanded Sam.

"No. That deputy hit it right. We may have trouble getting much of anything out of this Haskins character. But he belongs on this range, and he ought to know what we can expect. . . . He's the man to go to next."

"Could be. But I'm hungry, Stevens," announced Ezra. "And I'm tired too. I've had enough skirmishin' around for one day."

Pat was ready to agree. "Nothing much we can do tonight anyway. We'll pull away from town and make camp. We can eat and catch forty winks—and we'll tackle this Haskins party tomorrow morning."

It was fortunate for them now that they had brought their pack horse along, so that they were not dependent on the one restaurant in the Agency village. Ez explained that Haskins' Bar H lay half-a-dozen miles to the south, and they struck off in that direction. A couple of miles from town, just as the pale moon was beginning to show above the horizon, they found a brushy hollow hemmed about by rocks. Here they pulled up for the night.

There was desultory discussion of the situation as they got supper and relaxed over a smoke after eating. It seemed impossible to reach any decisive conclusions till they learned more about local conditions. It was highly possible that old Haskins might resent their unexpected return, especially after he learned what brought them.

There was even the bare possibility that, aware of having put over a crooked deal, he might have pulled up stakes and moved on. But this was remote. Ezra not only expected to find him but thought he would be able to make the rancher talk.

They rolled in their blankets, and all proved so healthily weary after a busy day that not even the oppressive silence of the empty desert disturbed their rest. As usual in this country, the temperature went down during the night. They awoke to a fresh and sparkling morning, and the mesquite wood fire felt good while they got breakfast and prepared to shove on their way.

Haskins' little Bar H spread, when they approached it an hour later, proved a miniature oasis in the mouth of a shallow canyon. A gushing spring in the rocks, which fed a tiny stream running for several hundred feet before it sank into the sandy soil, provided moisture enough to supply a little plot of greenery about the squat adobe ranch house. The leaves of an ancient cottonwood rustled cheerfully in the fresh morning breeze.

They came up to the place along the edge of a barren ridge, and Pat noted how arms of broken rock and detritus reached out to embrace the canyon's mouth, protecting it somewhat from view. A few head of cattle were in sight, browsing indifferently on mesquite beans; but probably the bulk of old Joe's stock was either hidden from sight farther up the canyon or scattered widely about the broken desert range.

They were drawing near, riding side by side and conversing casually, when a sudden harsh call jerked them to attention.

"Haul up there! Where do yuh think you're headin', out this way?" The voice seemed to come from somewhere in the tumbled rocks.

Pat quickly drew rein, muttering a warning to the others. "Watch this. There's a rifle barrel glinting over in those rocks—"

They halted, and for a brief time silence fell. Ez was the first to size up the situation. "Is that you, Haskins?" he hailed.

"What if it is?" came the crabbed retort. "Sheer off! There ain't nothin' I want from yuh—and yuh won't like the only thing I'm givin' away!"

"Hold on, old-timer," Sam interposed. "Don't yuh know us? It's Ezra and Sam Sloan. We got to talk to yuh." He started to push forward confidently.

"Who—?" old Haskins demanded suspiciously. "Better stay put, mister, till I figure yuh out—"

They saw the rifle barrel level rigidly, and Sam as hastily came to a halt once more.

"Told yuh to take it easy, didn't I?" he sang out boldly. "It's Ez and Sam—we just bought them roans from yuh, if yuh need remindin'!"

That had its effect. The rifle wavered and then slowly came down. "Sam and Ez, yuh say?" Haskins was clearly puzzled. "Then what are yuh doin' back here again?"

"Come on out here where we can talk," Ez roared with sudden vigor. "We don't neither of us bite—and this other man is a friend of ours!"

After a long moment Haskins appeared, stepping around the rocks and staring at them fixedly. He was a small, gnarled figure, and he must have been crowding seventy. He hadn't an ounce of excess flesh on him and still looked vigorous and alert. His brown eyes were genial by nature, and Pat guessed the deep lines in his lean face could fall as easily into a smile as into the stern frown he was wearing at the moment.

"Don't tell me you're lookin' for more horses," he growled, eyeing them keenly as he came forward.

"Not the same kind anyway," Ez declared. "We're lookin' for the same ones we drove away from here, Haskins."

Old Joe apparently had the habit of squinting one eye shut while the other grew surprisingly sharp. At this however, both flew open in a hard stare.

"How's that? . . . Don't tell me they got away on yuh," he barked.

Ez was watching him narrowly, asking himself if the man had any inkling of what had happened. "They got away all right." He nodded sagely. "In company with your highhanded Sheriff Lybolt and four deputies, as a matter of fact!" He waited for the effect this would have.

"Wha-at?" Haskins' tone was frankly incredulous. "Yuh can't mean Gif stopped yuh and took them roans away—?"

"Worse than that, old man." Ez related how he and Sam had thrown the posse off the trail, unaware of their identity, only to have Lybolt appear at the Bar ES.

"He swore them roans were stolen from Fort McDonald Army Post, Haskins. Wouldn't even look at the bill of sale yuh gave us. He reclaimed 'em for the cavalry— he said." Ez made the statement carefully, fully aware of its deeper implications and wondering what the reaction would be.

Haskins looked for an instant as if he had just heard that a favorite maiden aunt had been robbed of her crutches. "I will be danged," he declared in a furious tone. "Yuh mean that wall-eyed highbinder had the nerve to tell such a story as that—?" He was still frankly incapable of taking it in, and there could be little doubt of his sincerity.

"That's the reason he gave us, Haskins," Sam inserted flatly. "Lybolt swore the U S brand had been altered to an O8, with the H added. There was just enough chance he might be right so that we didn't give him too much argument till we found out exactly where we stood."

"Yuh stand to be took for a couple of prime suckers if yuh let him get away with that!" yelled old Joe. "Yuh mean Gif Lybolt actually ignored my bill of sale and took them broncs clean out of your hands—just like that?"

"We're down here tracin' 'em right now," Ez answered tartly.

The rancher's face was slowly blackening with fury. "That's the worst outrage I've heard in many a day!" he exclaimed bitterly. "Not that it's the first by a long chalk. . . . Gif Lybolt is nothin' more nor less than a double-barreled, ivory-handled crook, and a brassy one at that! He's workin' hand in glove with them other blacklegs there at the post, Sloan, if yuh got to be told. They're all in this Indian ring—and not content with stealin'

them redskins blind, they get away with murder! But this
is the first time I ever heard of his gettin' away with such
a raw game with law-abidin' ranchers. I swear I never
heard the like of it!"

5

AS HE LISTENED to the angry rancher's tirade Pat was
thinking that Haskins acquitted himself better than expected in the face of an ugly situation. His was no unfamiliar story in the Southwest, where the men in charge
of the broad but nearly empty Indian reservations constituted such law as there was.

With no one to check them it was a strong temptation
to officials to mulct their ignorant charges in a hundred
ways. Occasionally a luckless rancher got in their way
also; and while usually this moral rot did not extend to
Army officers stationed at these barren desert posts, it
was easy for the men in powerful positions to win their
confidence and hoodwink them.

"Then you're satisfied there is an Indian ring in exis-
tence here at McDonald, Haskins?" Stevens spoke up for
the first time in measured tones.

Old Joe whirled on him. "Don't ask me to prove a thing,
mister," he jerked out tensely. "But do yuh need any
further proof? Accordin' to Ezra here, yuh spent quite a
lot of time gathering just that!"

Pat was obliged to agree that their private observations
thus far only confirmed the rancher's grim reading. "As
a rule that kind of an outfit is careful to stay away from
the Army," he pointed out. "They don't want any more
attention attracted to their doings than they can help."

"It's your friends here that Lybolt is makin' sport of
now," retorted old Joe shrewdly. "They ain't Army, are
they—?"

"No. But the service *is* involved—if those roans were Government property at any time," persisted Pat. "Sam and Ezra picked up their bill of sale from you. And they say you had your own, because you showed it to them. . . . Where did you get proof of possession for those horses, if I can ask?"

"That don't mean a thing." Haskins was all the more vehement because he was stalling. "Lybolt's your thief, Stevens! He ignored the legitimate bill your friends was holdin'—and did *he* show anything to prove he was tellin' the truth? Yuh bet your life he didn't! I'm a little bit surprised at the lot of yuh for lettin' that fast operator get away with such a blazer!"

"Hold on, now." Despite himself Pat was amused by the old rancher's reasoning. "The U. S. Government is in a position where it doesn't have to prove anything. It places the burden of proof on individuals, Haskins; and when it comes to a combination of the Army *and* a sheriff's posse you just don't argue. . . . Gif Lybolt *is* a bona fide sheriff, I expect?"

"If by that yuh mean a connivin' schemer, I'll have to agree," growled Haskins sourly. "I reckon he was elected —after a fashion."

"I see." Pat nodded, wiping off his grin. "Usually a duly elected law officer makes pretty sure of his facts before he supports any claims. There must be some Army service back of those roans at some time or other. Where did you say you got your own bill of sale?"

Looking bilious at this cool persistence, Haskins showed no intention of offering a frank answer. "I don't much like your tone, neighbor," he rasped dourly. "Yuh wouldn't be accusin' me of some dirty work, would yuh—?"

"Why don't you tell him the truth, Pa?"

The four men jerked around as this clear, level voice broke in on them from the edge of the rocks. Pat touched his hat brim at sight of the slim, graceful and brown-eyed girl dressed now in trim overalls as if she had been working, who was obviously Haskins' daughter. "We got our bill of sale for those horses from Flint Lanark. We're not ashamed of that!" she continued with a trace of defiance.

"Hang it now, Libby!" protested Joe angrily. "Why can't yuh keep out of this and let me handle it?"

She glanced at Pat and his friends almost with hostility. "Don't talk as if we had anything to hide, then," she retorted impatiently. "You'll only make matters worse for yourself by seeming to. . . . Who is this man with Ezra and Sam?"

"Stevens is the name, ma'am." Pat's smile was faint. "We've just been telling your dad that Lybolt confiscated the horses my friends bought from him. . . . Who," he pursued in an easy tone, "would Flint Lanark be?"

"Why, he's—" She broke off suspiciously. "You're not a detective or an Army scout or something—?"

"Nothing like that," Pat murmured. "I run the Lazy Mare ranch in Powder Valley, up north of the line."

"A—rancher, you say?" She was still trying to figure him out. "Does your work bring you way down here, Mr. —Stevens?"

"You didn't hear me, I guess." His grin was engaging. "Sam and Ezra are friends of mine. . . . And I *would* like to hear who this Flint Lanark is?"

"He's an enlisted man over at the Army post." That was definite enough. "He's six foot, Stevens, with sandy hair and hazel eyes. Parts his hair on the left side—"

"Okay, okay," Pat protested humorously. "I won't need his brand marks, thanks. Just wondering where he hailed from." Privately he could not help reflecting that Lanark's identity as a cavalryman sorted well with Sheriff Lybolt's claim that the roans were actually Army stock.

She followed his thought quickly enough. "That's right. We were helping Flint sell surplus Army broncs, mister. Lybolt had that right enough." Libby was noticeably bold, daring him to find flaws in her story. "Where he fooled your friends was in pretending the Army had any further interest in them."

Pat heard her out, his brows raised. "Like that, eh? . . . Then the bill you got with those horses must have been signed by the post adjutant—"

They easily detected the direction of his reasoning. "Hope yuh don't think I'd have had anything to do with that horseflesh otherwise," Haskins interrupted flatly. "With me livin' right next door to the Army!"

"Wouldn't know till I asked," murmured Pat. "There seem to be others around who don't think that means much of anything. . . . What if I asked you for the loan of that bill of sale for a day or two, Haskins?" he queried tentatively.

Old Joe promptly shook a flat refusal. "Now I know there's a question about them roans—nothin' stirrin'," he said stoutly. "If Gif Lybolt or anybody else comes rampagin' out here askin' questions, Stevens, I'll be needin' that paper to shut 'em up."

"Lybolt as much as said you were holding a phony bill," Pat gave back casually. "He'd probably claim it was forged or something—"

"By hickory, it ain't!" exploded Haskins. "Lark told me he saw Charlie Widmark sign off that bill himself." He gestured vehemently. "Come on to the house. I'll show yuh!" He headed for the ranch house at a jerky trot.

Following him, Pat dismounted to walk beside Libby, while the partners single-footed in the rear. "Your dad has every confidence in this young fellow Lanark—I suppose he's all right?" he remarked to her.

"Flint?" She still did not feel absolutely sure of him, and her eyes flashed. "I'll back him any day, mister—and so will Pa."

He nodded. "Just asking. Because if Lybolt was on the level," he pointed out, "it looks very much as if somebody was trying to get your friend Lanark over a barrel."

Her eyes opened wide. "Why do you say that?"

"Why, if it comes to the point, either Lanark or that adjutant will be pinned down," he explained tersely. "And if Widmark *should* disclaim his signature, you can see where it leaves the young fellow."

"Faced with the charge of turning Army stock over to us for resale without authorization, you mean." The look of awakening dread on her face told him once and for all how young Lanark stood with her. Nothing more was said in the portentous silence as Haskins stamped into the adobe and came storming out a moment later, waving a crumpled paper.

"Here it is! All clear and plain, with the Government stamp on and Widmark's signature, plain as day!" he announced testily.

Pat had his careful look at the proffered bill of sale. It certainly covered the horses in question, and appeared in order as far as he could see.

"I suppose you're acquainted with this adjutant—saw his signature before, and it's all okay?" he asked idly.

Haskins paused. "Well—I've seen him, yes. Can't swear I've seen his fist before," the rancher said grudgingly. "But it *looks* just like him!"

It was flimsy evidence to go on. Pat shook his head. "Better let me take this, Haskins," he advised. "Widmark's acquaintances at the fort will know his hand, no matter what he says. I'll make it a point to check with them."

"I dunno—" Old Joe was strongly reluctant, reaching jealously for the bill. "I hate to let it get out of my hands. It's all the protection I've got, Stevens!"

"I'll make sure that you don't lose it," assured Pat. "But I'll be going to the fort anyway. And the quicker your innocence is established the sooner young Lanark will be off the hook. Surely you can see that."

"Let him take it, Pa." Libby made up her mind abruptly. "Stevens is on the same side we are. He's got to be if he hopes to get those horses back for Ezra and Sam."

Still old Joe hesitated. "Will yuh swear yuh won't let them hombres take this paper away from yuh?" he demanded uneasily.

Pat laughed. "Not unless we decide to throw the horses away for good," he declared lightly. "After all, this is the only real proof that any of us have a right to them."

This cogent reasoning had its effect. Haskins reluctantly consigned the paper to Pat's care. "Just make sure I get it back if it turns out I need it," he ordered. "What'll you be doin' now?"

"The first thing is to hunt up young Lanark and get his story," put in Ezra brusquely. "This whole affair seems to be boilin' down to a tangle between Lanark and Sheriff Lybolt. One or the other is bound to be lyin'. I'd just as soon believe it was that sheriff."

"Just don't shove over there to McDonald with a chip on your shoulder," warned Haskins gruffly. "Nobody blames yuh for wantin' your horses back; but the thing to remember is that the Army has things all its own way there on that reservation—"

Pat glanced up. "Then you're not on the reserve here?" he inquired quickly.

Old Joe shook his head. "I was a freighter in this country when things was really wild, Stevens. I got married and settled down on the Bar H before there was any reservation. . . . The line runs a mile or so north of the canyon here."

"You get along pretty well with the Indians, I expect?" Pat pressed curiously.

Haskins shrugged. "Except when they're on the rampage," he returned shortly. "I've had my ups and downs like everybody." He did not say what they had been.

There was more talk before the trio took their leave. It pleased Stevens that Libby Haskins seemed to have relaxed some of her suspicion of his motives. "We'll tell Flint you put in a good word for him," he smiled as they parted.

She flushed suddenly. "Don't you do that," she ordered. "Just leave my name out of it, Stevens—"

Pat pretended surprise. "Okay, I will," he promised. "If Flint Lanark is the kind I think he is, he'll know without being told. . . . And they call me Pat," he added.

Haskins himself pretended to pay little attention to this talk. "Don't forget I'll expect a report on what yuh find out, Stevens," he put in brusquely. "Not that I think it'll be much."

Pat nodded. "We'll be around a while," he predicted. He lifted a hand in brief farewell. "Be seeing you—"

Ez and Sam had their look at the little ranch as they rode away. "Snug little place at that," commented Sloan. "Haskins can hardly run more than a hundred or so head —and he probably has to make an occasional deal on the side, like those roans. But you'd hardly think anybody around here would get jealous of him."

"He's making a living and no more," Pat judged. "It satisfied me right away that he was probably honest enough."

"Could it be that somebody in that Indian ring is maybe after the Bar H?" Ez put in speculatively. "Accordin' to Haskins, any such game ain't rightly commenced yet— but I can see trouble headin' this way over them roans. They just ain't got around to it."

"That's right." Sam glanced toward Pat. "What is it yuh expect to get out of this Lanark party that we don't already know, Stevens?"

"I wasn't thinking of tackling him, right off anyway," returned Pat slowly. "It was Ez who gave Haskins that idea, and I let it ride. . . . I would like to get acquainted with the C.O. there at McDonald," he pursued. "Time enough for that too. Right now I'm thinking about those three strays we picked up—"

"What about 'em?" Ez prompted.

"I'm pretty sure that business was no accident," Pat thrust on. "It could be that we stumbled onto something we've no business to ignore. . . . If those strays were dropped deliberately," he proceeded thoughtfully, "it's ten to one somebody will come back looking for them. I'd be downright interested to know just who it is."

They looked at him alertly. "Say, yuh may have a point there," assented Sam. "Yuh mean we ought to shove back to that abandoned ranch—hang around a bit—and see just who shows up?"

"That's the general idea. Those strays are the best kind of bait, boys. And whoever comes hunting for 'em, it'll be interesting to watch what he does when he finds them penned in that old corral."

"What are we waitin' for?" Ezra's single eye glinted with anticipation at the prospect of action. He sat straighter in the saddle, urging his mount to a brisker pace.

Setting a course calculated to avoid both Fort McDonald and the agency, they set off toward their objective, which was nearly a dozen miles from the Bar H. It seemed a monotonous ride over this swelling, brush-tufted range across which dust occasionally swirled. Once they saw a mounted Indian at a distance, but he quickly faded from sight. It gave them the feeling of being constantly watched, whether or not this was the fact.

A few rocky buttes, studding the southern skyline, seemed scarcely to change their positions at all as they rode; but the rugged Colorado plateau to the north gradually drew near. It was still on the sunny side of midday when they spotted the bench on which the abandoned ranch was situated.

No sign of life showed in that quarter. As they drew closer the brow of the bench cut off their view. But Pat was now more interested in scanning the outspread desert country behind them. "Won't pay to let anyone else see us getting here first," he remarked. "We better follow that arroyo that curves round the end of the bench, and come up behind the place."

They rode into the rocky wash where the sun was broiling. Sweat stood on their faces and the air seemed dead. There was little talk as they climbed to the level of the bench. They came out at a brushy spot a couple of hundred yards to the rear of the tumble-down, abandoned ranch. Looking about alertly to make sure no one had preceded them here, Sam let out an exclamation of alarm.

"Why, there ain't a single horse in that corral now, Stevens!" he whipped out.

They saw at once that he was right. "Easy, now," said Ez practically. "Them bars are all busted down on one side. A wolf or somethin' could've spooked them broncs and they broke out. If that happened they won't be far away, and we ought to spot 'em right off."

They rode hurriedly toward the rickety corral. Ez warned the others back as they drew near. Dismounting, he walked forward with his keen glance searching the ground.

"Oh, oh." He motioned them forward, pointing. "Take a look at that—"

They saw now that someone had been here before them; someone who had deliberately torn the corral down and driven the roans out. Pat grunted.

"Too late, boys. Our friend beat us to it—whoever he was—and put the grab on those roans in a hurry. He's gone now. And so are the strays!"

6

"WELL, SHUCKS." Sam Sloan was royally provoked. "There must be some slick-fingered hombres on this range. We left them strays here only yesterday afternoon—and late at that!"

"Don't forget this is Indian country," returned Pat briefly. "You don't see much of them, that's true; but Navajos prefer to live in lonely places—and for all we know we're being watched right now."

"Then yuh think some redskin made off with them strays?"

"All I know is what I can read here." Stevens gestured toward the tracks in the dust. "Indians ride unshod broncs. The ponies that came here were barefooted. You figure it out."

"Whoever got 'em, they're still horses that we paid for." Ez looked at his young friend keenly. "What about this, boys?"

"Get to work, Ez. And don't be calling me 'boy'—"

"All of forty, ain't yuh?" snarled the one-eyed tracker sarcastically. "Just lay off the braggin', Stevens! Sam and I may be gettin' on, but I notice yuh still depend on us pretty regular."

Pat shrugged, tossing a wink at Sloan. "They're your horses," he retorted. "Do as you're a mind to about it."

With no more comment than an unsubdued snort, Ez set to work. It was not long before he picked up the track of the strays, which angled down an almost hidden trail at the other end of the bench. Apparently two riders had been in charge, and it soon grew plain that they had linked the captive roans together head to tail, probably by means of hackamore ropes, for easy leading. Ez called attention to the fact.

"This trail may lead us to some Indian wickiup in the desert, if we don't lose it altogether," remarked Pat, nodding. "We'll see."

The trail led down off the bench and out over the brushy level. Now and again the tracks virtually disappeared on flinty ground, but Ezra picked them up each time farther on. Whoever had confiscated the roans a second time had spent little effort in concealing their departure.

For better than an hour the way led across apparently empty wasteland. They reached an almost imperceptible crest, then the ground slanted downward. Still later they realized that a canyon lay ahead. Coming toward the end of the second hour to the sudden brink of the rocky crevasse gashing the level of the desert, they peered over into a gulf far deeper and wider than indications led them to expect.

"Why, say!" exclaimed Sam, peering downward. "There's a tiny creek down there. Grass too—"

"Yes. It's a ranch." Pat pointed out a handful of grazing cattle and, farther along the canyon, what looked like a work corral. The ranch house was not visible from this point.

The trail of the strays had turned east, following the rim of the canyon. It gave them their direction. Pursuing this course for another mile they saw where a little-used trail twisted downward into a ravine. The lead horses had gone that way.

"Hold on! That's a one-way trail," said Ez sharply as Sam started to push forward. The warning halted them where they were, and they gazed about. Just here the canyon wall was broken and eroded into a sinister area of weird pillars and crags, down through which the narrow trail plunged.

Hauling his mount aside, Pat sought for an unobstructed view downward into the canyon. A moment later he called out in a low voice. "Here you are. Get a load of this."

Moving that way they looked down through an accidental gap into the canyon. Far down on the floor, diminutive at this distance, could be seen a comparatively extensive ranch, with many out-buildings and sheds, and a snarl of corrals on the farther slope. Scanning the place with care, Ez finally pointed.

"That pen way over, with a hide hangin' on the top bar. Ain't them our roans in it, Sam?"

Sam peered attentively, then yelped. "Sure it is. Of all the nerve! Why, this ain't a dozen miles from where we left 'em, Stevens. . . . I see Indians down there too. Yuh don't suppose this could be a Navajo ranchero?"

Pat's headshake was firm. "No, some big shot must head a spread of that size. Those Indians may be working for him, and probably are." He started for the trail.

"We goin' down there?" queried Sam uneasily. "We'll be spotted before we get halfway, Stevens—and bold as them horse-snatchers are operatin', they'll have a hot welcome waitin' for us!"

Pat shrugged. "Say we are seen. So we're asking for work. You can't find it without going where it is." His tone was level and practical. "I still aim to know just who snagged those roans."

For a time they were forced to give all their attention to the descent. Such glimpses as they caught were only fleeting ones of the ranch below, but it was possible to note an unusual activity about the place, even from this distance. While it seemed inevitable that they should have been seen, as they came out on the last broad slope with the place spread out before them not one of the dozen or so men visible about the ranch paid them any heed whatever.

"Watch out for a setup here," growled Ez.

Pat made no direct response but his face was colder. He rode in the lead as they made for the sizable adobe ranch house, not missing a detail of their surroundings. An extensive yard stretching along the side and back of the house would have afforded a clear enough view of the corrals at fairly short range. But as they reached its near edge a middle-aged, stocky man in range garb came stepping out through an arched adobe doorway, gazing at them alertly. It was natural to turn their mounts in his direction.

The man's level gray eyes were stony with authority, his deep chest-tones gruff. "Help you gents?" he inquired curtly.

"Expect you could." Pat's nod was easy. "We sort of fell over this place here in the canyon. Whose spread is it, anyhow? . . . We're on the lookout for work," he added, as if that detail explained everything.

"This is Anchor, friend," was the reply. "You've heard of that? Belongs to Abe Crispel—Indian Agent at Mc-Donald." There was a note of pomposity in the inclusion of all this detail, clearly intended to impress. "My name happens to be Bradner."

He must have misinterpreted the promptness with which the brows of the Bar ES pair hoisted. Pat knew how to deflate him. "Bradner, eh? You must be Crispel's second fiddle—"

"No, that's Kip Thorne. I—don't expect Anchor is takin' on help just now," Bradner said hurriedly. "But Thorne does the hirin' and firin'. Come with me."

They could not help noting that he seemed to be herding them with some care as he led the way toward the front of the house, farther than ever from sight of the corrals. Dismounting, the trio followed after. At a niche in the rambling wall a modest door opened onto a small apartment. It stood ajar, but Bradner knocked formally on the weathered wooden casing and waited.

A tall, beady-eyed man in flannel shirt and flopping vest—as lean as Ezra himself but with Indian-black hair and scraggy black mustache—appeared briefly in the opening. "Yep," he rasped dryly. "What is it now?"

Pat stepped forward. "Howdy, Thorne. . . . The name is Stevens," he introduced himself genially. "My two friends and I are after work."

"Nothing just at present," Thorne retorted quickly. "What led yuh here anyway, Stevens?" His narrow-lidded gaze was curious. "Did somebody tell yuh about Anchor?"

Pat waved a hand. "No, we're crossing the desert and just sort of fell over it. . . . Kind of far between jobs in this country." He smiled.

"Better try elsewhere then." Thorne appeared ready to turn away. He shot a meaningful look at Bradner which plainly said: *Get rid of them.*

"You couldn't reconsider?" Pat asked. Thorne's headshake was dour and preoccupied.

"Not a chance," he grunted, turning away abruptly.

Bradner was waiting for them, prepared to ignore their expressions of disappointment. "Your best way out is straight up-canyon, boys." He pointed. "Only a few miles to the fort that way."

Pat shook his head. "We were figurin' on going the other way, friend—"

Bradner would have argued, but he caught himself. "Reckon yuh can if yuh have to. I'll show yuh." He turned to a saddled pony at a nearby hitching-post. "Come along."

As they struck down-canyon past the straggling length of the ranch they noted that Bradner seemed inclined to keep their attention occupied as they passed the corrals. But each of them took his casual look, and they learned what they wanted to know. Well beyond the ranch Bradner drew up.

"Road runs up the wall a mile down, on the right side," he advised in curt dismissal. "Yuh might find work over around Albuquerque—"

They watched his broad back as he turned and rode off. "Short about it—and not overly sweet either," observed Ez ironically, once the man was beyond earshot.

Sam paid little attention to the remark. He had been

waiting for the first opportunity to speak up. "Did yuh notice how quick them roans disappeared out of that back corral, Stevens?"

Pat's grin was humorless. "I noticed they kept us around in front of the house while they were moving them, too."

Ez glanced back with a snort of disdain. "Such doin's —and at the Indian agent's spread to boot," he growled. "Joe Haskins is dead right about this Indian ring! Crispel is doin' himself proud here. He must be breakin' the law a dozen ways. Shufflin' them Army roans around could be his biggest mistake, all the same . . . What now, Stevens?" he broke off.

"Well, we know where those strays went anyway. Probably they can be tracked down again in a pinch." Pat frowned thoughtfully. "I'm ready for that Army post now."

Ez nodded his agreement. "About time we got down to brass tacks, instead of all this poker playin'," he said testily.

They reached the road leading out of the canyon and climbed laboriously up to the rim. It was somewhere around midafternoon, the sun a brassy ingot halfway down the sky. The broad, well-marked trail led over the barren slopes.

"Haskins' Bar H must be somewhere along this road," Sam suggested, gazing about them.

Pat pointed to the rocky ridge knifing the horizon on their right. "That's the ridge behind his place, if I'm not mistaken. It won't be far out of our way—we might as well stop back and find out if Sheriff Lybolt's been there or if old Joe has learned anything more."

Reaching the faint turn-off, they followed it. This time the leathery rancher saw them coming. He met them in the yard, and young Libby stepped out of the adobe house as they drew rein.

"Did yuh get anywhere with that bill of sale, Stevens?" asked Joe abruptly, his eyes watchful.

Pat shook his head. "Not yet, Haskins. We're heading for the fort right now, as a matter of fact. I got to wondering if Lybolt showed up here yet—"

"Long as he got away with them broncs, he won't."
The rancher looked nonplused. "Why should yuh expect
anything like that, anyhow?"

"That's plain, old man. If we force him to cover his
own yarn through the Army, he'll be comin' back on you
for his proof," Sam pointed out bluntly. "If what you say
is true, Haskins, he'd rather drag you into his troubles
than admit he was wrong."

Haskins sobered immediately. Obviously this aspect of
the case had not previously occurred to him. "Thanks
for the warnin'. But if yuh go straight to McDonald, like
I thought yuh was doin', they'll soon tell yuh we're in the
clear. Let 'em deal with Lybolt in their own way!"

During this exchange Libby called Stevens aside with
a motion of her shapely head. "You're going to the Army
post now, Pat?" she inquired in a lowered voice.

Pat said yes. The girl displayed hesitation, but finally
spoke, shooting a quick glance toward her father. "Will
you ask about Flint Lanark—and make sure he's all
right?" she pleaded, her cheeks reddening.

"I sure will," he assented. "I intended to anyway. You
haven't seen him lately, eh?"

"Not since he turned over those roans to us." Her tone
was troubled. She would have said more, but Haskins
called Pat into the general talk and there was no chance.
From old Joe's comments it appeared he had no confidence in the officers at Fort McDonald, and he warned
them plainly to watch their step. Pat replied that he expected to. The trio left a few minutes later, promising to
relay word if they learned anything.

"Let's get on to that post pronto," said Ez as they set
off. "Once there we ought to know dang quick where we
stand."

Half an hour later they saw the buildings of the fort
standing out across the flats. The Army cantonment was
a scattered settlement, its various structures built around
the broad parade-ground. A knot of official buildings was
grouped at one corner, under massive cottonwoods. The
United States flag flapped fitfully from a tall pole.

It was not unlike other Army posts they had run across,

and they knew their way around. "We'll take a look in the sutler's store and ask a question or two," Pat remarked as they jogged that way.

Freighters, off-duty cavalrymen and civilians, with an occasional officer among them, made the post a fairly busy place at this hour when the heat was dying out of the afternoon sun. Pat noted the sentries posted here and there about the sprawling garrison. Dismounting before the sutler's store the three stepped inside.

Some non-coms were hobnobbing at one counter, their chesty Irish voices deep and resonant. An Indian stood staring fixedly at the saddle accoutrements hanging from the ceiling. The chief clerk was obsequiously waiting on a smartly attired captain at a cigar case.

Waiting briefly, Ez bought a plug of tobacco and then engaged the lank-haired underclerk in talk. "Must be quite a command here at McDonald," he observed. "Two full companies anyhow. How would yuh go about findin' a friend that lives in barracks—?"

"You ask for him," the clerk informed in a bored tone. "Sergeant of the guard'll know. Who would it be?"

"Young fellow named Flint Lanark. He's just one of the yellowlegs—"

The clerk looked up slowly, his gaze suddenly sharp. "*Lanark,* you say? Sorry. Can't help yuh."

Pat put in a word, calmly insistent. "Who should we ask?"

The clerk shrugged. "Don't know." He was suddenly anxious to get away. "If there's nothin' more you want—"

Ez would have collared the fellow in disgust on the spot. But Pat nudged him hard. "Let it go."

They stepped outside, looking the place over with new eyes. "Funny. You'd think Lanark's name was poison around here," Ez muttered.

Pat realized that some echo of the deal in roans must already have got about. They stood in the beaten dust, briefly undecided. "I suppose we could hunt up the adjutant himself—" Pat began.

"Wait a minute," Sam spoke up. "There's a gent I know yonder. . . . Hey, Rafe!" he called.

A lean, sinewy old fellow looked their way, flapped a hand, and after a moment came sauntering forward. Clad loosely in what looked like cast-off city clothing and a battered soft hat, he was straight as a ramrod, with faded blue eyes under straw-colored brows.

"Howdy, Sloan," he greeted in a markedly mild voice.

"Rafe Baker! What're you doin' here?" demanded Sam, slapping hands with him jovially.

"Just doin' a little scoutin' for old Van," was the modest answer.

Sam chuckled. That this old acquaintance from Leadville days should be an Army scout at McDonald seemed pure luck. "Just the man I need. Bake, we're hunting for a young cavalryman named Lanark," he announced confidently. "Where can we find him?"

Rafe tipped his battered hat back slowly. "Flint Lanark, eh? . . . Wait here, Sam."

He set off at his easy, long-legged stride. Sloan winked at his companions. "This'll do it," he predicted.

As a result of his assurance, none quite expected the news that came back fifteen minutes later. Baker reappeared, his homely face wooden. He was alone. As he stepped up, he shook his head soberly. "Yuh can't see Lanark," he announced flatly. "He's confined to barracks, Sloan. Somethin' about a charge of horse stealin'." His glance fixed meaningfully. "Sorry, but that's how it is."

7

AT BAKER'S portentous words the three friends looked at one another significantly. "There's your answer," Ez allowed with some gruffness. "Sounds like Lybolt was tellin' the truth after all. That don't look at all good for old Haskins."

"How's that?" The Army scout was mystified by their

talk. Sam explained briefly from the beginning. Baker listened with a faraway look. If the happenings up north in Powder Valley were new to him, he did not seem at all surprised by what had occurred here. Pat eyed him shrewdly.

"It's my guess you were called in on this deal, Baker," he offered. "You could maybe tell us a thing or two, for that matter."

Rafe's nod was brief. "I was ordered to find out where them roans went to," he declared. "No great trouble about that. Made my report—and I suspected young Lanark would be up on the carpet. The Army moves slow, Stevens—sometimes. Flint was only confined to barracks sometime today."

"He's due for a court-martial next, eh?" inserted Ez interestedly.

"I reckon. He'd probably be in the guardhouse if old Van thought it was downright serious," Baker added. "But he can't duck a hearin', no matter what."

"What kind of a man is your C.O.?" asked Stevens thoughtfully.

"Van?" Rafe spoke absently, his eye following a spit-and-polish cavalry captain who moved past them. "Lieutenant-Colonel VanOsdell, he is. . . . Oldish, and sensible in spots. At least he ain't one of these smart young whippersnappers!"

"A man can talk to him, then?"

"Oh yes." Baker hesitated. "But that ain't sayin' anything about persuadin' him, Stevens. I've had my whirl at that. Van can be stubborn as any other old line officer, and then some."

Pat nodded. From the rough-and-ready description he drew a pretty fair picture of the sort of officer Colonel VanOsdell probably was. "I expect he's available for consulting—"

"Keeps office hours," was the answer. "In fact, his wife is usually in a huff because he don't attend the dances and other post doin's."

"Much obliged, Baker. I want to learn more about

young Lanark if I can. We'll tackle the Colonel right now."

Baker pointed out the administration building, a rambling frame structure with a roofed porch running around three sides. "Van's got his office over there, where the guard can stall off Injuns and woodcutters," he said tersely.

They turned that way. The sentry at the door presented arms but did not offer to prevent their entrance. "Shall we wait out here, Stevens?" queried Sloan, awed in spite of himself by the military formality.

Pat waved them on in. "We'll all talk to the Colonel. I want him to have the whole story."

A clerk at a desk inside rose to meet them. "What'll it be, gents?"

"Want to see the Colonel, if he's in," Pat informed him. "It's about those Army horses," he added smoothly as the man gave signs of offering a regretful refusal.

"I—see." There was a quick change of attitude. "Just a minute, please. Colonel VanOsdell is in conference just now. I'll see."

He knocked at an inner door, slipped through, and was gone for some time. Finally he reappeared. "Take a seat there." He waved toward a row of straight-backed chairs against the wall. "The Colonel will be free after a while." He turned back to his desk and promptly forgot them.

"Can't say I like all this pussyfootin'," Ez grumbled to Pat as they sat down. "All these patent-leather Johnnies slip around like well-oiled ghosts—"

Pat only smiled. Little was said as they waited. It was late afternoon, the shadows long. Beyond a deliberate rumble of heavy voices coming from somewhere, the only sound in the room was the pronounced buzzing of a fly.

After what seemed a long delay the inner door abruptly swung open. A tall, rawboned individual stepped out, swinging his Stetson up. Pat saw at a glance that it was Sheriff Lybolt. Clearly having spent some time with the Commanding Officer, the lawman saw them sitting there. His eye raked them sharply. At the same time his stride broke, but he neither halted nor spoke, passing on to the door and out.

Ez looked at Pat, who shook his head as they started to rise, taking it for granted that Colonel VanOsdell was now at liberty. The clerk quickly intercepted them. "No, no, no," he said severely, warning them back to their seats. "You'll have to wait."

Pat shrugged, dallying with his hat as the man punctiliously knocked, gained admittance to the colonel's office again and closed the door after him. "The old Army routine," growled Sam.

After another delay the clerk opened the inner door and held it. "This way," he announced expressionlessly.

Pat was amply prepared for the blocky, grizzled and square-faced old campaigner who sat behind a rigidly uncluttered desk. Even here in his private domain, although the Colonel had removed his jacket and hat as a concession to afternoon heat, he was in dress uniform with his tie severely correct below the square-cut beard. There was a brooding heaviness in his ponderous glance, but it was plain he took in every detail of his visitors.

"Afternoon, gentlemen." VanOsdell's diction was clipped and precise.

"How are you, Colonel." It was Pat who spoke up, stepping forward. He introduced himself and his friends. "We came here to see one of your enlisted men, sir. Now I understand he's under detention." Pat paused.

"Ah?" The officer displayed no particular interest. "Who would that be, Mr. Stevens?"

"Young cavalryman named Lanark—"

VanOsdell lifted his heavy lids then. "Lanark, you say?" His hesitation was deliberate. "You've been correctly informed, I'm afraid. Unfortunately, your friend Lanark is not—available."

"Is there any possibility of reaching him, under surveillance for that matter, say for five or ten minutes?" asked Pat courteously.

VanOsdell started to shake his head. His frown was heavy. "Is there a legitimate reason why you must see Lanark just now?"

With no reason for concealing it, Pat nodded. "It's about those roans that Ezra and Sam bought." He briefly explained the confiscation of the horses in Powder Valley by Sheriff Lybolt, much as though the officer had never heard of it. "I don't know Lanark personally, Colonel; but I understand he was involved somewhere in the transaction. We feel we have a right to inquire into the circumstances."

The Colonel harrumphed. "I see. The horses were— bought in good faith, I take it?"

"Certainly—and as far back as we're able to trace, the proof of ownership seemed to be clear enough." Pat had no wish to drag Haskins into the picture by name until he had to.

VanOsdell drummed on the desk with blunt fingers. "It happens those particular circumstances are about to be inquired into, Stevens," he said abruptly. "Of course, the Government tries to be scrupulous where private citizens are involved." He thought for a moment. "May I see the bill of sale you received with the stock?" he asked the Bar ES partners directly.

Sam fished around awkwardly and finally came up with the soiled paper. VanOsdell spread it out and for a space sat motionless. "Hmm." Without speaking, he tapped a bell on the desk briskly. The clerk appeared hastily.

"Sir?" He saluted.

"Send in the corporal of the guard, Sergeant," Van-Osdell ordered.

The sergeant bounced out briskly, and the corporal was almost as prompt. Another snappy salute as he appeared in the door, and its perfunctory return. Ezra winked slyly at Stevens.

"Corporal, Trooper Lanark is confined to barracks," said the C.O. brusquely. "I want him brought here."

The corporal saluted and withdrew. This time there was a longer wait. Pat was much interested in the young cavalryman who marched in ahead of his guard. Libby Haskins' description seemed accurate enough. Flint Lanark was every inch of six feet, and he had markedly sandy hair and keen hazel eyes. But his air of forthright resolve, rather wooden in the presence of his Commanding Officer, had to be seen for itself. On the spot Stevens decided that Lanark was a likeable enough chap, or would be when he unbent.

Lanark came to attention before the Colonel's desk, saluting mechanically.

"At ease, soldier." VanOsdell's gruffness showed him not altogether devoid of human feeling. "Here's three men who've expressed an interest in you."

Lanark turned slowly, his eyes cold as he looked the trio over. "Never saw them before, sir."

"No, I guess not," VanOsdell said dryly. "However, two of them bought seventeen Army horses on the strength of a bill of ownership said to have passed through your hands. Perhaps," he continued as Lanark stared into space without speaking, "you'd care to explain."

"Is that an order, Colonel, sir?"

"Not at all." VanOsdell shrugged. "I merely make a suggestion for your own good. In a case like this investigation is inevitable, of course. Anything you can say or do to simplify it will count in your favor."

Lanark's hesitation was momentary. "Very good, sir. I can only report that I was ordered to dispose of the horses, and did so."

The Colonel's frown was a little incredulous. Clearly he thought this flat statement to be an evasion. "Come, now," he urged harshly. "Surely you realize that such orders as that can be checked from the adjutant's daybook?"

Lanark continued to gaze over his head without speaking.

"It happens that I have here the original bill of sale that accompanied those roans, Colonel," put in Pat, in an attempt to rescue the young fellow. "It bears the official stamp, and appears to have Adjutant Widmark's signature, all in order."

VanOsdell's delay was somewhat ominous as Pat started to fish the paper out. He extended a hand for it, and sat back, examining it deliberately. "Yes, yes." He looked up. "It does seem to be signed and verified by Charlie Wid-

mark. . . . Was this order registered, soldier?" he asked
Lanark.

"I don't know, sir." Lanark had shot Stevens a keen
glance of surprise at the appearance of the document. He
was once more woodenly noncommittal.

"It wasn't—and I'm wondering why." The Colonel
mused soberly. "You know that Mr. Widmark was transferred to Fort Bayard, Texas. The very day after this
order was issued, according to its dating. Of course it *was*
possible for him to have neglected or forgotten a routine
matter at such a time. But such things as these can
still be checked. I can even request the adjutant's recall if
necessary."

"Yes, sir." Lanark did no more than drop the colorless
acknowledgment.

"Meanwhile, pending a routine investigation it can be
said that we've recovered—ah—most of those roans."

"Most of them, sir?" Lanark was jolted out of his
stolidity.

"Fourteen, I believe." VanOsdell spoke precisely.
"Holding them until Widmark is able to untangle this
snarl *may* turn out to be just a formality," he pursued,
nodding in Ezra and Sam's direction. "Meanwhile, Lanark, if there's anything at all you can do to help us
locate the remainder, I'll be glad to reconsider your case."

"I, sir?" Young Flint was surprised again. "I—did hear
that Sheriff Lybolt recovered some Army stock. But you
will recall that I've been under house arrest since—"

"I know." The Colonel was almost tart. "Since one
of your fellow troopers reported seeing you driving the
animals in question." He spoke ironically. "My offer
still stands, soldier. Aid us in recovering the three remain-
ing horses, and I stand ready to—reconsider your situation."

There seemed a significance in his insistence which
brought a dull flush to Lanark's jaw. Stevens interposed
before he had time to speak up.

"Possibly I can help you there, Colonel," he offered
slowly.

"You?" VanOsdell stared. "It strikes me you'd be the last to help us reclaim that stock, Stevens!"

"I know," Pat nodded, allowing himself a faint smile. "Still it happens I've a pretty fair idea where those roans are, because I saw them only a few hours ago."

"So?" The officer's voice grated in sudden harshness. "Just where would that have been?"

"At Agent Crispel's ranch in the canyon," supplied Pat as briefly. "Anchor, I believe they call it."

VanOsdell's leathery face darkened in anger. "Mr. Stevens! Rance Crispel is a Government employee. Surely you're not trying to make game of us both——"

Pat gave him an innocent look. "Who, me?" He was markedly unruffled. "I'm not trying to do anything, Colonel, except tell you where those roans are."

The Colonel's testy manner did not soften in the slightest. "You must be mistaken," he declared distinctly. "After all, roans look a lot alike! I don't doubt Crispel may own some animals reclaimed from Army stock at some time or other——"

Pat only shook his head. "Not this time," he retorted confidently. "I appreciate your effort to correct me, Colonel—but I happen to know."

VanOsdell appeared to be struggling with contending impulses. "I presume you understand the seriousness of this matter, Stevens," he warned severely.

"That's right." Pat could put distance into his talk when it seemed advisable. "We've got Lanark's case to remind us if we're in danger of forgetting——"

The Colonel stilled, his features turned to iron. "Suppose you tell your story," he invited with chilling directness. Even Lanark was watching narrowly out of the corners of his eyes.

Pat told curtly how, following the confiscated horses south, he and his friends had picked up the three strays and turned them into an abandoned corral, only to find them gone later. "Ezra is as good a tracker as any you got working for you," he said bluntly. "He traced the strays straight to Crispel's Anchor—and we spotted them in a corral when we rode down there." He explained their small deception in asking for work, only to be turned off. "When we looked again, Colonel, those roans were gone out of that corral. But you can safely depend on it," he added shrewdly, "that they're still somewheres to be found right there on Anchor."

VanOsdell's face had grown mottled and craggy. "This is incredible," he burst out. "Hang it all, Rance Crispel is a friend of mine. . . . Sergeant!" His roar made the office door rattle.

The clerk appeared as if propelled by a spring. "Sir!"

"Get Lieutenant Crouse in here on the double," snarled the Colonel. In a matter of minutes the lieutenant himself pushed in, flushed with haste, but serene. He saluted, his eye sliding sidewise to take in the other occupants of the room.

"Lieutenant, I want you to throw a detail of twenty men into the field immediately," rumbled the aroused C.O. "You will proceed to Crispel's Anchor ranch without out a minute's delay. There may be somewhere on the ranch three roan horses branded HO8 at present. You will seize the said horses and deliver them to the fort at the earliest possible moment. I want a report the instant you return. Are your instructions clear?"

Crouse clicked his heels, saluting smartly. "Thank you, sir." He did not appear at all surprised.

"Very well. Proceed at once, Lieutenant."

A bugle sang its clarion call seconds after Crouse's departure. VanOsdell paid no further heed, turning to Pat gravely.

"Of course you'll be guests of the fort, Stevens, until the Lieutenant reports," he advised significantly.

8

Summarily dismissed by Colonel VanOsdell's brusque finality of tone, the three friends returned to the open. Ez was muttering to himself. "He's got his gall, Stevens —as good as warnin' us not to leave till *he's* satisfied we're not lyin'," he groused.

Pat took the matter lightly. "I wouldn't take that too seriously, Ez, if I was in a hurry. Right now we can afford to wait," he allowed. "Because I'm as anxious for results as he is."

Sam pointed across the parade. "There's Baker goin' in the sutler's," he announced. "Maybe we could squeeze some more out of him."

They moved that way. Sam entered the store to accost the scout, and they came out together. They joined Pat and Ez under a spreading cottonwood.

"I take it yuh reached old Van?" asked Baker calmly, delaying till he had gnawed off a chew of tobacco which he tucked in his cheek.

Sam assented, and Stevens briefly described the interview. The scout listened carefully to every word about young Lanark, whom he appeared to know and like.

A trumpet pealed down at the barracks while they talked. The order, "Prepare to mount. Mount!" drifted to their ears, and a moment later a small cavalcade swept across the parade-ground and struck into the desert beyond the post laundry and blacksmith shop. Rafe Baker watched with slitted eyes in the waning evening light.

"So this is Shiner Crouse's party, eh?" he murmured bleakly.

Pat pricked up his ears. "Know the Lieutenant, do you, Baker?"

Rafe's shoulders rippled in a lazy shrug. "Well as I

want to. He's a cocky bird. Waves his tailfeathers kind of high."

Pat resumed his tale about the strays, last seen on Agent Crispel's ranch in the canyon. Baker's chuckle was dry. "Crispel had 'em, you say?" He did not sound surprised. "Then somebody's lyin'. Lybolt swore he couldn't trace them strays. I got the impression they never was with that bunch he picked up. Reckon Van figured that way too—"

"But he did turn the fourteen head over to the Army?" Pat was particular on this point.

Rafe nodded. "Early this mornin'," he declared. A calculating look crept into his eyes. "You men picked up them strays directly behind Lybolt, did you?" he pursued.

Sam explained the exact circumstances under which the three horses had been found. Baker shook his head. "Don't hardly seem as if that could be an accident," he said flatly. "Yuh got Lybolt's statement to lean on if there was any question. . . . It looks to me," he mused, "pretty much as if Flint's got a mighty busy enemy."

"I gathered that." Pat's response was measured. "In fact, this whole deal is crooked. But I wanted somebody else to say it first."

"I'm sayin' it." Rafe's eyes twinkled coldly.

"Baker," Pat began seriously, "you know Army procedure better than any of us. But it struck me just now that VanOsdell pretended to be a lot denser than he really is. I seemed to gather that he's doing a certain amount of stalling. Would there be anything to that?"

The scout gave him a shrewd look. "You're catchin' on fast," was his terse comment. "Of course Van *could* be in the dark too, playin' it slow till he makes sure. But the old Army game never changes, Stevens. Never had any use for it, myself."

Pat nodded his comprehension. "What about this Adjutant Widmark who was so conveniently transferred?" he asked. "Even if he's gone he must have left records behind. The Colonel wouldn't even accept his signature on Haskins' bill of sale," he added.

Baker threw out a hand. "Don't know nothin' about

service red-tape, Stevens," he declared simply. "I do my work, take my pay, and let the shavetails make out the reports."

There was no help for them here. But the rough-barked scout had given Pat a valuable insight into various matters. He was interested because he knew Lanark personally and approved of him, and more particularly because he was an old acquaintance of Joe Haskins. There was an excellent chance that Baker might yet be of use.

The scout talked for another ten minutes and left. Thanking him, Pat promised to keep him posted on events. Later the trio procured several cans of peaches and a bag of crackers and cheese from the store, eating their supper on the edge of the sutler's porch. They wanted to be handy the minute anything developed; and Colonel VanOsdell's pointed interest in them gave them license to learn all they were able.

Evening closed down. Mess call had long since been sounded, and the hour calls rang from sentry to sentry around the fort. The cavalrymen emerged from barracks for brief relaxation, some visiting the sutler's, others gathering in knots at a safe distance from the officers' quarters or making for the lantern-lit stables.

Sheriff Lybolt was not to be seen again and probably had left the post. Soft lights gleamed in a score of buildings, and a subdued hum of evening activity could be heard. Darkness thickened, the stars came out, and an hour passed.

Not long before taps the trio heard a challenge from somewhere across the dark parade. The guard sang out. Almost at once they picked up the unmistakable sounds of a group of horsemen. "That's this Crouse comin' back," exclaimed Sam. "It didn't take him long, whatever he did. He'll be turnin' up down at the corrals," he pursued, starting to move off. "I'll edge down that way and find out what the story is."

Pat let him go, preferring personally to keep Colonel VanOsdell's cottage under surveillance. The C.O. had turned that way soon after the detail's departure, and

Stevens was confident the lieutenant would turn up there with his report in a matter of minutes.

Sloan came hurrying back through the darkness, his breath short with the importance of his news. "They picked up them strays," he announced. "I seen 'em bein' turned into a pen down yonder! Might've heard some of the talk down there, only a guard turned me back."

"Good." Pat nodded. "We'll just step over to Van-Osdell's and be ready when he wants us."

"Hold on, boy." Ez was still healthily cautious around this Army cantonment. "There's bound t' be a guard over there. He'll run us off—"

Pat laughed at him. "Think the Colonel's afraid of rats, do you?" he twitted. "We've got VanOsdell's word for it that we're wanted."

They moved that way. No one accosted them, and they were standing near the Colonel's cottage when gravel grated sharply under brisk boot heels and a stalwart figure moved up the walk, mounted the steps and knocked at the screen door.

After a brief moment the C.O. appeared, bulky and deliberate. "Yes? . . . Oh, it's you, Lieutenant." There was a cursory exchange of salutes. VanOsdell held the screen open.

Crouse moved in. For a second the Colonel stood in the opening, peering into the night. He saw their shadowy figures. "Who is that?" he demanded.

"It's me, Colonel—Stevens."

"Well, come in." VanOsdell was tersely hearty. "I want you to hear this, Stevens."

Since they already knew what they would hear, the trio stepped forward with alacrity. Lieutenant Crouse was waiting just inside. The Colonel waved toward the sitting room where a glass-globed lamp burned on a center table. VanOsdell said nothing as he plodded to a convenient chair and sank into it, facing them.

"Well, Russ?" He addressed his query in a tone that said military formality would be relaxed tonight.

Crouse waved a dusty pair of campaign gloves which

he had just finished stripping off. "Reporting the return of three roans branded HO8, sir," he said briefly.

The Colonel's hooded eyes flared up. "Found them, eh? I suppose there's no question about—" He paused.

"They're Lybolt's strays, Colonel," the lieutenant assured briskly. "There are now seventeen horses in Corral Four, all branded HO8."

VanOsdell nodded. "What did the Indian Agent have to say about them?" he pursued evenly.

"Agent Crispel hadn't been home for two days, sir," was Crouse's answer, to the Colonel's obvious relief. "Cape Marshall, his foreman, knew nothing about the roans and swore they weren't there. I had already located them at a rock corral in the upper canyon. We rode past the spot, closing in on Anchor." The young officer's tone was smoothly self-congratulatory. Obviously he was convinced of having pulled off a coup, and wanted his Commanding Officer to recognize it. "I talked to Thorne, Crispel's manager. Thorne thinks that one or more of his hands may possibly be involved. He has promised to investigate at once."

"I see." VanOsdell nodded sagely. "Very good, Russ. Very good."

"So where does that leave young Lanark, Colonel?" Pat struck in quietly. "I think it clears him of either complicity or evasion in this particular case—"

"Not at all." To the trio's surprise it was Crouse who interrupted boldly. "Lanark still stands charged with absconding with accredited Army stock—if I'm not mistaken, sir?" He turned suavely to VanOsdell.

Pat's silence gave point to his disgust as he gazed at Crouse attentively. The Colonel looked vaguely annoyed. "The original charge is not affected, Stevens," he said hardily.

"Not—?" echoed Pat.

"No. Lanark's story appears to hold together, provided he is telling the truth. But only Adjutant Widmark can confirm that—as we all know."

"And Widmark won't," put in Crouse smugly.

Pat ignored this, still looking steadily at VanOsdell.

"You can recall that adjutant, of course," he objected mildly. "But his records here at McDonald must show plainly enough whether or not Lanark is lying."

The Colonel showed a trace of embarrassment now. He was in no hurry, framing his reply with care. "As it happens," he confessed unhappily, "we're—not in a position to consult his records."

Pat leaned forward, sensing that at last they were getting to the bottom of this mystery. "That's mighty unusual, to say the least," he commented dryly. "Don't tell me Widmark left here under a cloud and the War Department requisitioned all his papers—"

"Why should you ask that?" Lieutenant Crouse seemed to be taking a lot on himself in the presence of a superior officer. But Pat knew that an indulgent C.O. often let his staff favorites get away with plenty. Already Stevens was privately questioning Shiner Crouse's motives.

"Because if Widmark himself had been caught in irregularities, you hardly need to look further for a culprit in the present case," he pointed out bluntly.

VanOsdell shook his head. "Nothing of the kind," he denied stolidly. "Widmark had nothing whatever against him here at McDonald. As you observe, that *would* simplify matters, Stevens; but it just happens that the adjutant's records have—unaccountably disappeared."

It was not the first time Pat was reminded that Flint Lanark appeared to possess an active enemy, and one not only diabolically resourceful but fully determined to make him as much trouble as was humanly possible.

"So you have that to cope with. . . . It must be plain to you, Colonel," Pat said, "that this couldn't possibly be Lanark's fault. Certainly *he* had no access to the adjutant's papers; and if they've been abstracted—at a remarkably convenient time for somebody—you'll have to look elsewhere in this case for the guilty party."

"That's . . . true," assented the Colonel slowly. It was Russ Crouse who shook his head knowingly.

"Not necessarily, Stevens," he objected reasonably. "It's known that Lanark has friends here at the fort. Why isn't is possible that he used his influence to make sure

those papers disappeared—especially if there was anything in them not in his favor?"

Pat noted absently that the lieutenant was talking only
partly for his benefit, watching carefully at the same time
the effect of his words on VanOsdell. He refused to argue
the academic point.

"We're going backward now. In circles," he declared
firmly. "I'll confess I'm not familiar with Army usage. But
my understanding is that a man is considered innocent
until proven guilty. Lanark doesn't seem to enjoy that
privilege. . . . Or am I wrong there?" He glanced up
keenly at the Colonel.

A grim smile touched VanOsdell's mouth. "In the
Army, Stevens, except for a gross misuse of authority we
pretty much consult our own sense of justice. You've made
a point, though, that I can hardly ignore altogether." He
was unbending remarkably for an officer of his standing,
perhaps partly because he was aware these men might
yet prove the legitimate owners of the horses in dispute.

Pat alerted. "Does that mean you'll restore Lanark to
duty?" he queried.

"It means I'll parole him until Adjutant Widmark's
recall can be effected," was the reply. "Lanark has not indicated to me his personal concern over this tangle. But
as you point out, it could be a great mistake not to afford
him the chance of straightening it out." He paused.
"Would you consider acting as parole officer, Stevens?
I've inquired into your status," VanOsdell admitted candidly, "and find you to be a responsible person."

Pat had no intention of appearing anxious, despite the
unexpected opportunity to relieve Libby Haskins of great
concern. "As Lanark told you, Colonel, I don't know him
personally. I came down here," he stipulated frankly, "in
the hope of helping to drive those roans back to Powder
Valley where they belong."

VanOsdell's nod was perfunctory. "As I pointed out,
I'm afraid I can't help you there until Widmark returns.
Orders have been cut for his recall," he confided. "And
it's just a matter of time."

Pat shrugged. "Under the circumstances we'll wait."

"Does that mean you'll—" The Colonel paused.

"Be responsible for Lanark, you mean? Something depends on exactly what *he* thinks about it," returned Pat shrewdly. "Why can't he be restored to duty as usual?"

"Because until Trooper Lanark has been acquitted of wrongdoing his rights and privileges are being withheld." VanOsdell turned to Crouse. "Tell the sergeant to have Lanark brought here, will you, Russ?"

The lieutenant left, shaking his trimly barbered head as if unconvinced. It was some minutes before Flint Lanark once more put in an appearance, followed closely by his guard.

VanOsdell returned their salutes and spoke to the guard. "That will be all, Corporal. Your charge is being admitted to parole."

Lanark's head jerked up and he looked about. His critical eye seemed to pass over the Colonel without seeing him. Meeting Pat's grin, the young fellow had no difficulty in attributing his good luck to the other. So stringent had been his training that his mouth opened and closed without speech.

VanOsdell grunted, tugging at his rugged mustache. "Did you have something to say, Trooper?"

"Excuse me, Colonel—sir." The words tumbled past Lanark's stiff lips. "Did I understand you to tell the guard I'm on parole—?" He waited keenly for the reply.

"I've asked Stevens here to be—responsible for you. You're expected to pay close attention to his instructions, and to reappear before me on order. Is that fully understood?"

"Yes, sir. Thank you, sir!" Lanark spoke crisply, red with some suppressed feeling. Snapping his boot heels, he saluted again and whirled to Pat. "At your pleasure, Mr. Stevens, sir!"

"Relax, soldier . . . Pat'll do." He gestured in the direction of the door. "Let's get ourselves out of the Colonel's hair for a spell."

"Stevens," VanOsdell spoke up as they turned to leave. "I regret to inform you that a report of Indian activity has reached me within the last hour. It *may* amount to nothing here in the north. However, I recommend that you use care in moving about the open range—"

"An Indian uprising?" Pat's frown was surprised. "I thought these Navajos were considered peaceful, Colonel?"

The officer nodded slightly. "They are. It's the Mescaleros who are off the reservation, in Arizona. Sometimes they prowl this far, raiding my peaceful Indians for horses—and attacking anyone who happens to get in their way." He lowered his voice. "This information is not to be broadcast. But you are warned."

"Thank you, Colonel. We'll be careful." Pat signalled to the others, and Lanark marched out followed by Ezra and Sam. Stepping into the open, Stevens noted Lieutenant Crouse watching from the doorway of the nearest cottage. Crouse stared hard for a moment, then turned away. Unless Pat was much mistaken, the cocky lieutenant disapproved highly of this whole proceeding.

9

"So you're my superior officer now, Stevens," remarked Lanark as they paused in the company street. There was an edge of challenge in his voice, faintly derisive, as if the badgered cavalryman suspected some ulterior motive. "You're not a detached Army scout or something, are you?"

Pat said, "No, I run the Lazy Mare ranch a couple of hundred miles north in Powder Valley. Ez and Sam happen to be friends of mine."

Lanark was still mystified. "How did you work it?" he queried bluntly.

"I didn't. Your colonel more or less shoved it at me." Pat's smile was reserved. "We're chiefly interested in just what did happen to those horses, soldier, and we still aim to get them back."

A defeated look stole into Lanark's eyes. "I expect you know the whole story by this time——" he began.

"Pretty much of it. But not enough," Pat admitted candidly, "to understand it altogether. VanOsdell seems to feel there's something queer about that deal. He may be hoping I'll get something out of you that'll explain it."

"I don't know what it could be, Stevens!" There was desperation in the young fellow's tone. "From the time I was suddenly confined to barracks I haven't heard a thing. You probably know more right now than I do."

"Could be. . . . Let's get our broncs and clear out of here," interrupted Pat abruptly.

Lanark broke stride. "Where we goin'?" he demanded.

"We'll make for Haskins' Bar H first."

"Well—hold on." Flint was uncertain. "I don't know how glad they'll be to see me again, Stevens——"

"Don't worry," Pat said firmly. "Libby and her dad are on your side. At least they sure were the last time I talked to them."

Lanark showed relief. But he hesitated. "I can't depend on using an Army bronc," he objected. "Way things are now, it kind of puts me aground."

Sam made little of this. "I'll borrow a pony and saddle from Baker," he put in. "He was around a while ago. That's probably him sitting over there on the sutler's porch steps."

Sloan walked across and spoke briefly with the scout, then they moved from sight in the soft darkness. Sam was back in short order, leading a saddled bronc which he turned over to the trooper. "You've got a friend or two left, whether yuh think so or not," he observed shortly.

Lanark swung astride, waiting while the others got their horses. They set off. Not till they had left the fort behind was anything more said. Finally Ez spoke up. "I'll tell yuh our story, Lanark," he began gruffly. "Yuh can go on from there—if yuh want."

Flint followed in silence the tale of their having bought the HO8 roans from Haskins, and how they had evaded what they thought to be stock thieves, only to have the horses confiscated by Sheriff Lybolt at the Bar ES.

"Fourteen of 'em, I guess you mean?" the young fellow interrupted. "How *did* you lose three of them?"

"That's another story." Ez told how Lybolt had commandeered all seventeen of the horses, how they had trailed the posse south and picked up the three strays on the way. Lanark expressed considerable indignation.

"Somebody lied," he charged forcibly. "I was accused of knowing too much about those strays! Why?"

"Because somebody was interested in keeping you in trouble," inserted Pat. "We got that right away, Lanark. I was wondering if you might know who it could be?"

Flint snorted. "I'm obliged to you for bothering even to that extent," he acknowledged, ignoring the query. "Nobody else seems to have!"

"Keep your shirt on. We're still interested in your story —if you want to tell us."

Flint's delay was long. "Nothing much to it," he declared finally. "I'll say right off that those roans *were* Army stock, of course. Haskins doctored the U. S. brand into an HO8."

Pat grunted. "Been safer if he'd just vented the Government brand and put his road brand alongside, wouldn't it?"

"Expect so. But there's a story behind that too—"

The trio waited.

"I've known Joe Haskins for many years," Lanark began. "He started his Bar H and ran it for a long time; and he was pretty prosperous in his day. Some years back, during an Indian uprising, a lot of Army stock was show down or stolen, and Joe's horse herd was commandeered. Most of it was lost or ruined during the long campaign— and for some reason his claim to be paid for that stock was disallowed. They said he waited too long or something."

The three listeners said nothing. They had all heard such stories before. Certain hardshell Army officers were notoriously hard on ranchers. Once they moved on in the endless rotation of transfer, little could be done.

"I felt sorry for Haskins," averred Flint. "Expect I've even got a reputation for crabbing about it around Mc-Donald. Once it was plain that Joe's demand for reimbursement was thrown out, I—well, I tried to square it for him."

"Then yuh *did* put the snatch on them Army roans without permission?" interrupted Ez harshly.

"No, no! I had orders from Widmark to dispose of those broncs," Flint protested doggedly. "I knew he was being transferred. I sold Haskins the roans for almost nothing, Stevens—I figured he could recoup some of his loss. And I waited till Widmark was gone before I reported the sale," he confessed. "Probably *that* was my big mistake. Old Joe thought if he altered the brands there'd be less chance of the stock being traced. Seems we didn't either one of us figure right," he concluded gloomily.

Pat could not help but agree. "You realize of course that Widmark is being called back here to testify? If he backs you on one point, he's bound to condemn you on others. Seems to me you left yourself wide open, Lanark."

There was more talk, but Flint stubbornly refused to yield his position. "The Army gypped Joe Haskins," he said flatly. "I tried to do what I could for him. If they throw the book at me, that's it."

"What about this Lieutenant Crouse?" asked Pat. "He doesn't seem to be wasting any love on you."

Lanark thought about this, but seemed not to take it seriously. "Crouse hardly knows I'm alive," he judged.

"You never tangled with him in any way?"

"Oh—I guess he took Libby away from me a time or two at post dances. That don't mean anything—"

"Why don't it?"

"It was just show-off," Lanark insisted. "I'm sure of it. Crouse is rich, I understand. He'll marry in society, as he calls it, and he's just playing around out here."

Pat kept his own thoughts on this to himself as they thrust steadily across the desert. The lights of the Bar H presently came into view, reminding Sam of something.

"What about this Apache scare VanOsdell was tryin'

to throw into us?" he asked. "Haskins has got a mighty lonely place here. We tellin' him about it?"

Pat weighed this before answering. "No point in worrying Libby needlessly," he opined. "Haskins is an old hand at this stuff—and we'll be around for a day or two. Is that your opinion, Lanark?"

Flint agreed. "Keep the broncs close to the ranch—and both eyes open," he said tersely. "Apaches aren't interested in cows. Joe don't have anything else."

"Better not let him get you talking about those roans, either," reminded Pat. "Until this is straightened out, the less said the better."

Flint grunted. "Warn him, Stevens—not me. Right from the start I've been scared to death *he'd* get involved in this business. As it is, I figured he wouldn't want anything more to do with me."

"Nothing like that. Just tell him you're waiting now. Ask him if you can't stay there at the ranch for a few days —and we'll make our headquarters there."

When they rode into the little spread twenty minutes later, however, Lanark hung back, pretending to take care of the horses while Stevens made their presence known. Only when Pat called to him did he come forward.

Haskins and Libby were in the kitchen, talking after their supper. They invited the four men in, and Libby poured coffee for all. Pat was interested to watch the meeting between Lanark and the girl. Oddly enough, she greeted Flint casually, and it was he who showed diffidence.

"Well, Stevens! Did yuh get them horses back?" was old Joe's greeting.

Pat said they must wait pending some routine investigation by the army. "We thought we'd spend our time here if it's agreeable to you—"

"Why not?" The rancher was hospitable. "Long as the yellowlegs don't come after us, with Lanark here!" He was cheerful enough to make a joke of sorts out of it.

"No, I borrowed him for a while," explained Pat as easily. "There was something about three strays that Sheriff Lybolt couldn't account for. I told the Colonel where they could be found, and that squared us with him—"

"What? What's this about strays?" The rancher had not been told the story, and he listened cynically while Sam explained. At the end he snorted his disdain. "I declare, I don't know what this range is comin' to, with a crook behind every rock," he growled sourly, totally unconscious of the ambiguity of his own position.

"What do you know about Lybolt?" asked Pat curiously. "Is he a little on the stupid side, or what?"

Haskins flashed him an angry glance. "I told yuh," he retorted doggedly. "Gif is on the side of this Indian ring. I call that stupid, smart as Lybolt is in some ways!"

Letting it go at that, Pat could only hope the unfolding situation would not involve the Haskinses in the morass of either state or post politics. The talk became general; and he observed that while Libby did not deliberately avoid Lanark, she seemed determined to keep him at arm's length.

Stevens was offered a room in the ranch house, but young Flint escaped with relief to the barn, accompanying Ezra and Sam. The silence of this desert country was intense, almost palpable; and if more than one of the four men remembered the warning they had been given about Apaches, night passed without disturbance of any kind.

Awake early next morning, Pat found the girl up before him, making breakfast in the dusky kitchen. "It was fine of you to look after Flint," she said to him directly.

"Nothing to it. Let's say I did it as much for you as anything," he replied lightly.

Her slight stiffening was barely perceptible. "Please don't—mistake my interest in Flint, Pat," she said strictly. "He is an old family friend, of course. It's just that I—we hate to feel responsible."

"Oh?" His surprise at her attitude was only mild. "I'll try to remember that." He smoothly turned the talk as Joe Haskins appeared, adjusting his galluses.

"Well, Stevens! I see you're no slugabed anyhow," the rancher rumbled. "Yuh ready for us, girl? I'll get the others out of the hay—"

He had barely reached the kitchen door when he beheld
Ez emerging from the barn, followed by Sam and Lanark.
"Come an' get it, soon as yuh wash up," he bellowed.
"We don't throw nothin' out!"

Breakfast was a silent affair. But when they gathered
in the yard afterward, keenly aware of pearly dawn light
and the pure thin air, all were brisk enough. "What'll it
be today, Stevens?" inquired Sam officiously.

Pat's smile acknowledged the little man's urgency.
"Why, I was thinking about—" He broke off, his glance
running level across the gray desert. "Looks like we'd be
having a visitor first thing."

Gazing that way, they made out the tiny moving dot
his keen eyes had picked up. There was no thought of Indians now, since these would never have shown themselves
at all. Yet suspense unconsciously tightened them up as
they waited. Long before the advancing rider came within
hailing distance Pat recognized the Army uniform. Ez
was only a second or so behind him.

"Hanged if that ain't this Lieutenant Crouse comin'!"
he burst out harshly.

Lanark's lean face became cold and closed, and the
others fell equally silent. Only Libby, who came to the
door at that moment, appeared to notice nothing unusual.

Crouse rode forward without swerving in the slightest,
and they read in this the directness of his purpose. He
jogged into the yard, touching his fatigue cap to the girl.
Then he dismounted and turned to face the men. "I'd like
to know just what brought you here, Stevens," he declared
coolly, with a show of authority.

Pushing his hat back, Pat appeared faintly amazed.
"Mostly because I took a notion to, I expect. Does it
make a difference, Lieutenant?"

Crouse obviously had no intention of allowing the situation to get out of his hands. "Attention there, trooper!"
he snapped at Lanark. "Step aside. I want a word with
you—"

As he spoke he walked to the edge of the yard, and it
was a moment before he noted the dead silence and

Lanark's failure to comply. "Did you hear me, soldier?"
He raised his voice sharply.

Though he saluted mutely in the presence of his superior, Flint remained stubbornly where he was, his glance
sliding uneasily to Stevens. But it was Ez who spoke up.
"Don't be puttin' on the dog with them shoulder straps,
Crouse," he warned roughly. "We know you're playin'
the officer! I don't happen to be an enlisted man and I
can tell yuh what we all think of yuh—which is not
much!"

Crouse stiffened up at the insinuation that he was taking an unfair advantage by pulling his rank. Ez continued
to jab at him shrewdly. "We all know Lanark's been relieved of duty and paroled to Stevens—and it's mighty
nosey of yuh to tag along after us," he proceeded hardily.
"Without that official dignity of yours yuh might not be
so brave!"

"Ezra," came Libby's icy voice from the house, turning
them that way. "You've no right to speak in such a manner. The Lieutenant is a guest at the Bar H," she continued pointedly, "and so are you!"

"Never mind. Anything to accommodate." It was
Crouse who responded sarcastically, his movements swift
as he methodically tore off his jacket bearing the emblems
of rank and savagely turned his shirtsleeves back. "All
right, Lanark! This is man to man. . . . Step aside, I said
—before I drag you!" He started forward angrily.

Lanark stiffened, his face dark. For a bare second he
had trouble taking this in. Only when Sam propelled him
forward with a push from behind did he rush to meet his
advancing tormentor.

"Flint! Russ!" cried Libby tightly. "Stop it this instant!"

Neither heard her. Apparently a fair match, they came
together solidly with fists swinging. In that first savage
flurry the blows were almost too swift to follow. But suddenly Crouse threw up his arms and went over backward.

Lanark ran in, his fist poised. As Crouse started to
struggle up it caught him flush alongside the neck, spin-
ning him end over end to sprawl in the dust. Following
like a panther, Lanark hit him three times more, till the

officer was all but out on his feet. Lanark appeared scarcely to be winded.

Knocked lengthwise once more, Crouse rolled away to scramble up hastily and stand swaying. Flint closed in remorselessly, a punishing blow poised. Crouse saw it and shielded his face with an arm. "No!" he choked. "I don't —need any more—!"

Not once during the encounter had Flint opened his mouth to speak, nor did he now. Almost carelessly, his contempt plain for the other's fatal softness, he knocked Russ flat again, then turned away.

"Now that's what I call a job, boy," exclaimed Ez gutturally. "Maybe the lootenant has still got business here!"

Crouse dragged himself up, dazed and only outwardly subdued—bitterly chagrined over this decisive defeat before the watching girl. Reaching his horse, he pulled himself astride. "I—asked for that, Lanark," he gasped, still thick-voiced with rage. "But that don't change what'll happen to you the day Widmark gets back! Just hold yourself ready—because the next time you see me you'll be getting your orders!"

With this weak threat he turned his mount and started blindly away.

10

"THAT WASN'T SO smart, Ezra," Lanark said uneasily as they watched the Army officer ride off across the desert flats.

Ez showed surprise. "No—?" He looked around. "I thought yuh handled that bird pretty neat!"

"You know what I mean." Flint was curt. "Crouse must've rode over here on some errand. We never gave him a chance to name it. You needled him and he got mad—and like a fool I fell for the chance to plaster him good!"

"Forget it, boy," Pat put in calmly. "As Crouse had pointed out to him, you're in my custody now. I answer to Colonel VanOsdell only—unless it bothers you about what that glorified messenger boy will do when you're reinstated."

Still not mollified, Lanark looked dubious at these derisive references to the luckless lieutenant. He relaxed finally, and it was largely by accident that Pat noted Libby Haskins had turned back into the house. He forced a chuckle. "You don't think that character cuts any ice with her, I hope?" he jibed lightly.

Flint had no intention of giving his private feelings away. "It's got so I don't know what to think," he growled.

With scant respect for the Army or its minions, old Haskins cut into their talk brusquely. "We ridin' the canyon today or ain't we?" he demanded. It had been decided that they would help the rancher to police his range by driving the stray stock back down out of the hills. Old Joe had not been told about the Indian scare, but it was possible he knew, since many old-timers seemed to have a sixth sense about such things.

"Sure. We'll shove off now and get started," said Pat quietly. Getting up the broncs, they started out. Within the next hour Pat noted that the canyon supported a surprising number of steers. But if the rancher owned any horses at all he was holding them elsewhere. Pat commented on this fact.

Old Joe shook his head dourly. "The Army'll never take any more broncs from me," he averred flatly. "I was made a fool of once. It's why I sold them roans, Stevens, almost the minute I got 'em. Yuh know yourself, if *I'd* held 'em another week it would've been me that lost 'em!"

"Oh, yes. . . . No hurry about it," put in Sam. "But we meant to discuss that with yuh, Haskins. What about the money we gave yuh in good faith for them horses?"

Joe shrugged. "If I still had it I'd feel duty bound to hand it back till this business is straightened out, Sloan," he returned, averting his eyes. "It happens I paid off a small mortgage with that money—"

"So where does that leave us?" Ez fired off huffily. "I'll just remind yuh, Haskins, it's *your* bill of sale that was protested."

"Wait a minute," interrupted Pat. "We've got Lanark's word for it that the transferred adjutant duly authorized the sale of those broncs. If this can be proved, VanOsdell is bound to return them. He can't help himself. As soon as Widmark is recalled, we'll know for sure. That's plenty time enough to start any proceedings."

"And meanwhile we wait around with our teeth in our mouth," grumbled Ez discontentedly.

"No—I've thought of other angles to run down," Pat said. "We know now that the C.O. is not altogether to blame for Lanark's headaches. I can hardly tell him he's being bamboozled by some interested party—but I can look around myself, and I will."

"Where?" Lanark queried sceptically.

Pat spread his hands. "You just sniff around asking questions," he supplied. "For one thing, I'm ready now for a private talk with Sheriff Lybolt. Think I'll shove on into town this afternoon and hunt him up."

"It won't be healthy for me to show too much of myself just now," warned Flint. "Out of sight—you know."

"No, you'll stay here," Pat told him. "You and Sam can put in the time helping Haskins with his work. I want Ez along with me."

They returned to the ranch toward noon to have dinner, making silent note of the fact that Libby was an excellent cook. Afterward Pat and the tall tracker set out in the direction of Fort McDonald.

"Wonder if there's been any reports of them Apaches around here?" Ez mused aloud as they rode.

"We'll soon know," Pat responded. "It suited me to leave Sam and Lanark there at the ranch, just in case."

They discussed it in desultory tones. An hour later the scattered buildings of the Indian Agency came into view. Ez looked that way speculatively. "What do yuh expect to wring out of Lybolt now?" he asked as they reached the edge of town. They passed a Navajo hogan or two, where dark-faced children scuttled immediately from sight.

Pat smiled. "I can't be sure, of course," he admitted. "This is a fishing expedition, Ez. I'll ask questions and try to tip him off balance. I want to tackle him alone this time," he added. "But there's one job you can do—"

"What's that?"

"That tough posse of his. I've been turning that bunch over in my head. Wander around town, Ez, and keep your peepers open. If you spot any of that bunch, watch them, will you?"

Ez grunted, getting his point. "Still wonderin' just who they were, are yuh?" He broke off. "One or two of 'em could be ridin' for Crispel's Anchor outfit, at that."

They dismounted at a hitch rack running along one side of the trader's big store. At this hour, with the sun broiling down, only an Indian or two was in evidence, standing motionless and not missing a thing. A dog lay curled asleep in the hot dust, and from somewhere nearby came the bang and clatter of a freight wagon being unloaded. Cheery voices could be heard exchanging rough banter.

"There's a few saddle ponies around," murmured Pat. "Take a look in those saloons while I hunt for Lybolt."

They parted, and Pat moved into Gundel's huge supply store. Half-a-dozen leather-faced men were here, several talking together in low tones while they leaned against a counter. Pat wondered if they were discussing the Apache uprising, but he was unable to catch any words. A shirt-sleeved clerk was waiting on a woman in puff-sleeves and flat straw hat, who may have been an Army wife. A Navajo stood staring at the turquoise displayed in a glass show case. As he bought a sack of tobacco, Stevens glanced around. He and the clerk were alone at the moment.

"Where would I locate the sheriff at this time of day?" he asked idly.

The clerk shrugged. "If he ain't workin' he might be down at the Bourbon Bar—or at Lindauer's Livery—or he might be home. You'll have to hunt around, neighbor."

Pat nodded his thanks. Stepping out a moment later, rolling and lighting a smoke gave him time to look the street over. He spotted the ornate scrollwork sign, LINDAUER, in chipped paint over a stable entrance; and at that moment Ezra stepped out of the saloon a dozen yards beyond. He made a signal, taking his black flatbrim off and re-setting it at a cocky angle. Stepping off the porch, Pat sauntered toward him.

They halted a few feet apart. "Lybolt's in that stable talkin' horse," muttered Ez out of the corner of his mouth. "I ain't spotted them other hombres at all—"

"Keep looking." Pat spun his cigarette over his shoulder in an arc and walked slowly to Lindauer's gangway door. He stepped in, his eyes slitted against the shadowy gloom. Sheriff Lybolt and two other men were lounging against a stall siding, critically examining a trim bay held by a wizened cripple in torn overalls. They glanced up, and it was a moment before anyone spoke.

"You again?" Lybolt grunted then, tossing a whittled splinter away.

Pat's assent was cheerful. "Howdy, Sheriff. Like to talk to you a minute if I may—but no hurry. I can wait."

It was his way of indicating that he preferred to speak to the other in private. Gif got it. He glanced toward his companions and back, his dour air of authority once more apparent. Asking himself what this visit meant, he made up his mind quickly. "Something on your mind, Stevens? . . . All right, spit it out."

Pat pretended to glance about the stable in surprise. "Oh. Didn't know this was your office—" He paused innocently.

Lybolt stared fixedly and growled his irritation. "Gettin' official, are we?" Clearly he was in no mood to be put to any trouble for a comparative stranger.

Pat merely waited. As he expected, this forced the lawman to reluctant action. "We can go outside, I suppose, if this is a private matter," Lybolt conceded grudgingly, stepping slowly forward.

Ezra had prudently disappeared from view as the pair moved out into the street. Gif strode heavily around to the shaded side of the livery, where a weathered sawhorse offered a seat. Lowering himself deliberately, the sheriff shot Stevens a keen glance. "Well—"

"Since you'll find it out anyway, Lybolt, I've been named Lanark's parole officer pending investigation," Pat informed him quietly. "You must have heard that those three strays turned up and he's been released until Adjutant Widmark gets back here."

Lybolt was aware he had Pat to thank for his own chagrin where the strays were concerned. "You know a lot, don't you?" he said belligerently.

Pat's grin was disarming. "Just a happen-so this time," he deprecated. "I'm still wondering who's got it in that bad for young Lanark, though. Who all was it you had in that posse anyhow, Sheriff?"

Lybolt did not miss the left-handed reference to Lanark's betrayer, whoever he was. He glared his affront. "That's my affair," he brought out sharply. "Just what are you drivin' at, man?" There was an edge of hostility in the flat question.

Pat's shrug was casual. "Just checking things out by elimination," he returned coolly. "Because Powder Valley, Colorado, doesn't happen to be your bailiwick, Lybolt; and that was where I watched you pick up those roans—although my friends held a bill of sale for them."

The lawman's shrewd eyes widened at this view of events, only to narrow again craftily. "I don't know just what construction yuh put on that—if the U.S. Army is satisfied," he grumbled mildly.

"Oh—it's what happened afterward that interests me."

Lybolt looked stubborn. But he was cornered and knew it. "Oh well." He pretended indifference. "My boys are okay, if that bothers yuh."

Pat's nod was nicely judicious. "That's your opinion, of course—"

Lybolt showed anger at this persistence. "Like that, is it?" He snorted. "Ask around if Brad Lines ain't straight as a string, Stevens—and Mark Hamblin too, for that matter. Colonel VanOsdell will tell yuh! Or Rance Crispel, the agent, since he's right here in town."

"No doubt. That's two of them, Lybolt, besides yourself . . ." He paused expectantly.

"Go to hell, Stevens!" The sheriff leaped up from the sawhorse with new authority. "I won't be whipsawed by you or nobody else!"

"The thief hasn't been tagged yet for sure, Lybolt," Pat returned evenly. "As a law officer, I figured you'd be thankful for all the help you could get."

"All right now! I know my own job, and I'll run it." Gif retorted swiftly, starting to turn away. "Just don't stick your long nose too deep into things that don't concern yuh!" He barged off.

Pondering the interview briefly, Pat tucked the two posseman's names into his memory. Lybolt's flat refusal to name the last two seemed sufficient proof that he was intent on shielding their identity. Probably the two he had named—Lines and Hamblin—would prove above reproach. Just where Pat might obtain information about the others was uncertain. Either those named must be safely beyond reach or they had been warned to keep a tightly closed mouth.

Reaching the street, Pat saw Ez idling in the doorway of the saloon opposite. Farther upstreet a band of Navajos were pulling up before the Agency building. Recalling Crispel, the agent, Pat considered briefly his quick glimpse of the other. He thought the man would prove harder to pump, if anything, than Lybolt.

The midafternoon hush was broken by the clop-clop of a pony. Glancing around Pat froze, suddenly recognizing the rider. He was the blocky posseman with a slight cast in one eye who had roughly warned them away from Fort McDonald on the evening of their first arrival.

The man spotted him. Turning abruptly in at a hitch rack, he dismounted to loop his reins over the rail and stand fumbling with his saddle gear. Pat knew the other was warily watching him.

"He's one of that crowd—and probably neither Hamblin nor Lines." Pat debated whether to move directly for-

ward and accost the fellow. But Lybolt himself was somewhere near at hand; and moreover, the burly puncher's actions gave him his cue. Pat shrugged. "If I don't keep
him in sight he'll probably do the same for me," he concluded shrewdly. "Let's see just how far we can get with
this."

He strolled across to his own mount tethered beside
Gundel's supply emporium. Pausing briefly to tuck the
tobacco he had bought into a saddle pocket, he glanced
up guardedly under his hatbrim. The blocky man had
moved out to where he could watch, apparently busy with
a smoke. Pat snorted softly. It was all he needed to know.

Striding casually to the other saloon in order to avoid
Ez, who seemed thus far to have escaped observation,
Pat stepped in and purchased an unopened bottle. Thrust-
ing this into a back pocket he re-emerged, making
straight for an open alley, trusting his watcher to draw
his own conclusions.

The alley ran between Lindauer's large barn and a ramshackle shed. Walking nearly to the far end, Stevens
turned abruptly—to observe the burly posseman purposefully following. Standing bottle in hand, Pat managed to
show disgust as the heavy-set man bore down on him.
"What you after, a free drink?" he brought out gruffly.

The other did not speak, halting half-a-dozen feet
away. He must have been badly surprised by the flashing
grin on Pat's face. Whirling too late, he saw lanky Ezra
blocking the mouth of the alley behind him. He understood instantly.

With a snarl he wheeled back toward Pat, his Colt
streaking out of the holster. Pat was too quick for him,
hurling the liquor bottle hard. It smashed against the
rising gun and knocked it to the ground. The bully
squalled, waving his cut hand in agony.

Closing the gap at a leap, Pat gave him no time to call
for help. A looping blow to the jaw spun the big fellow
around. He sprawled down, and Pat's lusty kick ruined
his effort to surge up on his feet. With a bellow he rolled
over, coming to his knees with the savagery of an em-
battled grizzly.

At that moment Ez's arm closed about his windpipe from behind. A single wrench brought an expression of desperation to the heavy, flushed features. He struggled briefly, then gave up. "Lay—off," he gurgled. "You're breakin' my neck! I ain't done nothin'—!"

Ez hauled him up, still captive, and Stevens eyed him freezingly. "Who are you?" he asked softly.

"The name is—*agh*—Grimes," the man wheezed. "That's all I know. . . . Let me go, can't yuh!"

"Grimes, eh?" Ez gave another stout squeeze. "Come on, Grimes! Out with the rest of it."

"I'm . . . Cade Grimes, Stevens! I'm just a—puncher!" The man was scared now, eyes starting out of his head. "I don't know a thing, I tell yuh!"

"Who else was in that posse?"

"Brad Lines—and Hamblin—and Gif Lybolt . . . *Ow!*" He gasped harshly, wheezing now. "Don't yuh bust my —Adam's apple!"

"Brad Lines—Hamblin—Gif Lybolt," Pat droned. "There must have been at least one more, Grimes. . . . Who was the Army officer along with you?" he demanded suddenly.

Grimes' bulging pupils blinked. He was past the point of gathering his wits speedily enough. "I don't know," he gasped in terror. *"Ow!* . . . It was—Lieutenant Crouse," he managed weakly, then slumped forward.

11

"Well, well." Ezra gazed down at the blacked-out Grimes unfeelingly. "Yuh never know, do yuh?" he marveled sardonically.

Pat showed no surprise whatever. "I had a pretty good hunch. Crouse has been altogether too busy to suit me," he grunted. "The question is—"

"Yeh," agreed Ez as he broke off. "Just how far *does* this go? Is the Colonel wise to all these shenanigans or not?"

"Lybolt had to know, of course. I see why he's been giving me the brush-off. But VanOsdell. . . . I'll give him the benefit of the doubt till I know different, Ez."

Leaving Grimes where he lay, they moved to the mouth of the alley, reconnoitering before they stepped into the street. Deliberately casual, they walked up the street then and crossed to their horses.

"Lybolt named a couple of that posse," Pat remarked. "But neither Cade Grimes nor Shiner Crouse. I got the impression he was trying to hide plenty—and how right I was."

Ez glanced about wearily as they stood between the horses. "Nothin' funny about an Army man bein' in that posse, for that matter. But why in disguise?"

Pat shook his head. "Can't say offhand—except that Crouse gave himself away by acting so cocky. He's so damned smooth and sure of himself. That ride with Lybolt out of uniform *could* have been a little idea of his own."

"A hombre like him usually gives himself away sooner or later," suggested Ez shrewdly.

"He has—and he will." Pat glanced at his companion briefly. "Tell you what, Ez. Take a trip over to the fort, will you? It won't pay to get too nosey over there—but make friends with Rafe Baker. He won't talk, and he can help us out plenty."

Ezra saw the plan, and gave a nod. "Keep an eye on Crouse for a while, eh?" he seconded. "Find out just what he is doin' with himself—"

"That's the idea. If he leaves the post at all, try to learn where he goes, and what for. Will you do that?"

Ez waved a big hand in a gesture of reassurance. He started to swing into the saddle. "I'll find the rest of yuh on the Bar H, I expect?"

"Unless something turns up. We'll leave word."

Ezra turned his horse toward the desert and seemed to fade from sight in the smoky heat haze almost at once.

Pat was in no hurry as he turned back into the street and rode quietly on his way. Even if Grimes reported his experience to the sheriff or to anyone, which was unlikely, Stevens did not expect it to go any further.

It was a hot ride across the baking flats in the full blaze of the afternoon. A gusty wind whipped up occasional sheets of bitter dust that made a gray mirage of the flats. Pat was well enough pleased to reach the sanctuary of Haskins' canyon.

The rancher was working about the corrals and Sloan was helping him. Pat saw Flint Lanark sitting disconsolately on the doorstep of the ranch house. "What's his trouble?" he asked when Sam came sauntering over to where he was off-saddling.

Sam showed his snag teeth in a grin. "Reckon it's his way of courtin' Libby," he supplied. "Only she don't go along with it. I noticed her coolin' off after that smooth Crouse hombre was over here—"

Pat's brows rose, then he grunted in comprehension. "Maybe it's natural she should be interested in his kind, at that. Lanark would have done better to let the lieutenant clobber him, eh?"

"Wouldn't say so. In my book, she's pretty well sold on that brass-polisher already."

"Oh well." Pat was not seriously concerned. "This is one way the young folks keep each other interested. She'll come around after she's put Lanark in his place," he predicted.

But Libby showed no inclination to do so. At suppertime, when she could no longer remain out of sight, she proved decidedly frigid to the luckless cavalryman. If she had any interest whatever in his reaction, Flint's gloom must have gratified her. Yet she was adamant, cutting off his hopeful remarks to her and pointedly leaving him out of her talk.

"I hope you didn't lose Ezra there at the Agency," she said to Pat as she filled his coffee cup.

Under the circumstances it would not have been politic to name the lanky tracker's true errand. Pat's answer was casual. "No, I set him a little chore there in town. He'll be along in a day or so."

"Set him to watchin' Lybolt, have yuh?" put in Haskins shrewdly. "Always thought that hombre was shady. Lately I'm gettin' sure of it."

Pat passed it off without comment, allowing them to place their own construction on his first remark.

Ezra did not appear till the following night, riding in shortly after dusk. He found Stevens sitting on the top rail of the corral with Sam. No one else had as yet noted his arrival.

"Here, are you? . . . What's the story, Ez?" Pat tossed his smoke away, waiting.

Ez rode close, reining up within a few feet of them. "Hated to come away at all, with that Crouse on the loose," he growled. "But so far, Stevens, he ain't been away from the fort except for a trip or two to the Agency. Seems to be messenger boy between old Van and Crispel—"

Pat was by no means disappointed in this report. "Did you find out anything at all about Crispel?" he queried.

"He's from Missouri. Baker says he was some kind of small-time politician. There was somethin' about his riggin' an election—"

Pat's smile was dry. "It figures. . . . Just keep on watching Crouse for a while, Ez," he directed. "And don't overlook that there may be more between him and Crispel in these official visits than appears on the surface."

Ez was perfectly aware of the fact. They talked longer, the tall redhead admitting that he had heard nothing at all in reference to young Lanark. It was known the order had gone out for Adjutant Widmark's recall, but no more. Half an hour later Ez slipped off into the night just as Flint Lanark banged out of the ranch house.

Pat met him on his way to the barn to turn in. "Tough luck, Lanark," he said sympathetically. "Won't she talk to you at all?"

"She did tonight." Flint's response was grim. "I could've done without all she had to say, Stevens." He was forcing the words out against his will. "Maybe you better take me away from here—"

"Keep your shirt on," advised Pat. "She'll cool off if you don't crowd her too hard. I'll have a talk with her myself, first chance I get."

"Don't you do it!" Lanark was vehement. "If I can't get anywheres with her myself I don't want to."

"Okay." Pat let it rest there. But the following day he made it a point to keep an eye on events at the ranch and observed the girl's determination to drive into the Agency town alone in the ranch rig to shop. She quickly brushed off Flint's diffident offer to accompany her.

Pat made his casual appearance in the yard shortly before she left. "Going to town, Lib?" he remarked. "Why not take Sam along? He can pick us up a few things and can help lift the heavy stuff."

"Not at all." She was exercising her feminine prerogative to remain firmly contrary. "Give me the list. I'll bring back what you want."

Lanark was watching jealously from a distance, so Pat did not argue. He named a few items and handed over the money. Libby whirled briskly out of the yard as if provoked with their pretense of supervision.

She was gone longer than usual today, apparently grasping her opportunity to extend her privacy. There was little change in her manner of lofty coolness when she drove in an hour before dark. If no one except her father commented on the lateness of supper tonight, she somehow managed to make him appear unnecessarily testy.

Ezra rode in while they were eating and calmly took a seat at the table. His brief response to queries indicated that all seemed much as usual at the fort. "They're movin' a bunch of Indians that seem too anxious to stray off the reservation," he reported. "Lots of bugle blowin' and ridin' around but no excitement."

Pat did not miss the casualness with which Libby asked if Ez had happened to be in town that day. She seemed relieved when he said no.

After supper the tall man waited his chance and drew Pat and Sam aside. "I lied to that girl," he announced significantly. "I *was* in town long enough t' see what she was up to." He paused for effect.

"Shucks. That's easy." Sam loved to take the wind out of his tall partner's sails, and his eyes glinted now.

"Yeh? So how was it?" snapped Ez.

"Why, she went ridin' with that brass-button Romeo," guessed Sam. To nobody's surprise, Ez nodded grudgingly.

"That was it," he acknowledged sourly. "I don't like it, Stevens! Crouse is makin' a fool of that nice girl—"

Sam was inclined to the same opinion, but Pat brushed their concern aside. "Libby's smart enough," he opined. "Sooner or later she'll see through Crouse—and for all I know, she may now." He paused. "What else has our busy-brained lieutenant been up to, Ez?"

There was little more to report, beyond the fact that Russ Crouse appeared to make himself as familiar around the Indian agency as at the fort. Pat thought it over soberly.

"He hasn't offered to take a ride out to Anchor yet?" he asked. At Ezra's headshake he went on. "That'll come next. Be sure and let me know when he does, will you?"

It was this warning which alerted Ezra to something that happened later that night after he had resumed his unbroken watch at Fort McDonald. For several nights he had been accustomed to watching in the dark. Largely by accident he saw the light go out in Crouse's cottage at an unusually early hour for the late-retiring officer.

Stealing close in the gloom, Ez presently heard a door open and close stealthily. Knowing what this meant, he was careful to get the emerging figure between himself and several dimly glowing post lights across the parade-ground. A single glimpse amply identified the broad shoulders and jaunty bearing of Russ Crouse, who was off on some quiet expedition of his own.

At the same time there seemed something unusual about Crouse's appearance. Ez risked discovery to get a closer look at him, then grunted. "Out of uniform again, huh?" The significance of this flashed through his mind. "We'll just make sure we don't lose yuh this time, mister!"

Delaying only to make certain that Crouse was heading for the corrals, Ez reached his own horse. He had to wait for several minutes, making sure he did not run into the guard, before he detected the quarry's quiet departure. Fully as competent to avoid the sentry as Ezra, Crouse rode past at a distance of a dozen yards and headed out across the flats.

For some time Ez depended on faint sounds and the thin acrid taint of dust hovering on the still air to enable him to follow his man. He dared not draw up too close lest Crouse should rein in and wait in silence to surprise pursuit. For twenty minutes he worked forward as fast as he thought wise. But the time came when the wary tracker was convinced he had lost the other altogether.

His alarm grew. Stevens was depending on him now to make sure of the meaning and objective of this clandestine night excursion. But almost at once a faint paleness on the horizon brightened to a thin silver glow. The moon peeped over a serrated range crest miles to the east.

The light slanting across the ghostly flats was deceptive. It threw deep shadows in the washes and magnified the brush clumps to monstrous size. But as he peered keenly from a rise Ez spotted a moving blot far beyond. As soon as it passed over a swell he hurried forward. Although unable to keep a close surveillance over Crouse, at least he was in no danger of losing him altogether.

For a time Ez concluded from the direction taken that the officer was making straight for Crispel s Anchor spread. A black slash of deeper shadow marked the canyon's course between silver-crowned buttes a few miles ahead. But Crouse swung away, avoiding the canyon. Wherever he was heading, it was not toward Crispel's. Ez silently admitted his blank puzzlement.

Half an hour later he knew. "Hang it all, with them civvies he's wearin' how come I didn't guess all along? That smooth buzzard's makin' straight for Apache Crossing!"

This was the isolated supply store and saloon, tucked in a shallow canyon a dozen miles west of McDonald, which Ez and his friends had run across in their search for the

roan strays. Although strictly off-limits, the place drew
the more reckless Army element, as well as desert drifters
and a few owlhoots, and according to Haskins it had a
decidedly unsavory reputation. Ez was so confident of his
objective that he swung away from Crouse's trail and
made directly for Apache Crossing under the cover of
rock-fanged ridges. Its name abruptly reminded him of
the Indian uprising mentioned by Colonel VanOsdell.
The isolated supply store would make a perfect target
for marauding Apaches. Here they could strike suddenly,
burn and pillage and pull away, with literally no danger
of being surprised.

The thought did not cost him a moment's qualms. Long
ago he had learned that when Apaches struck it was always in daylight, usually in the dusk or early dawn. If
they were here now, this was the time for rest or lying in
wait, believing as they did that the dark hours belonged
to the spirits. Ignoring any danger from that quarter, Ez
pushed boldly forward. He descended a rugged slant into
the ghost-shadowed canyon, drew up in a clump of post-
oak a couple of hundred yards from the tiny settlement
and tethered his bronc. He had scanned the place sharply
enough in daylight to enable him to approach quietly
from the rear.

Store and saloon were housed in one long, rambling
log-and-plaster building which had already sagged a little
out of shape. The racket of a tinny piano drifted from
open windows, and Ez caught the raucous voices of several men. Stealing along a side wall, he reached a grimy
paned window and crouched to peer inside.

Three or four hard-faced characters were carousing
about a frowsy woman pounding the piano. A lank-faced
sheepherder from the hills was holding forth loudly to
the bartender. And in a shadowy corner two men sat with
their heads together.

Ez watched for long moments before determining that
Russ Crouse was one of them. It was a jolt, when the
other man glanced toward the light momentarily, to recognize Cade Grimes. "Stevens was dead right," Ez grunted

softly to himself. "He knew that pair would be gettin' together. He was only wrong in guessin' where."

He drew back with a jerk as Crouse glanced directly at the window, but apparently he was not seen. For a long time he watched with bated breath as the stealthy pair conferred. Obviously their talk engrossed both. At one point the officer reached into a pocket, and Ez was reasonably sure that money changed hands. Grimes was giving the other a shrewd attention that said he was listening to orders.

Ez weighed this dourly. "Crouse ain't done with his dirty work yet," he concluded. "The question is—how to get next to his game?"

He was still pondering when an interruption occurred. One of the tipsy range men at the piano stumbled over to accost the two at the table. Crouse waved him away, without success. With cowardly bluster Grimes sprang up threateningly. But Russ quickly put a stop to this.

"He's too smart to call any attention to themselves by lettin' a row get started," mused Ez bleakly. His guess was confirmed a moment later when Crouse allowed himself and his companion to be urged toward the bar. Once there, a round was set up. The dreary, forced gaiety of the place seemed to gain a new lease on life. Ez was not in the least surprised to see the lieutenant joining in the boisterous laughter of the others, and as another drink was set up he even put his arm over the woman's sleazy shoulders in companionable fashion.

Ez drew back from the window to peer through the dark silence of the canyon, then hesitated. "Stevens ought t' know about this," he reflected. "If he wants to do anything about it, now is his chance!"

There seemed every likelihood that, their business transacted, Crouse and Grimes were good for another couple of hours of hilarity in the bar. Swinging away, Ez ran cautiously for his horse. Once astride, he swung away and set off at his best pace for the Bar H.

12

PAT STEVENS, who had been holding himself ready for just such a call, wasted no time on questions when Ezra rode into the ranch at a late hour. He routed out Sam, and made no objection when young Lanark signified his intention of accompanying them.

They saddled up and got away fast. Ez explained the situation as they sped through the night, and although Flint pricked up his ears Pat had little to say.

"What about this, Stevens?" the trooper demanded harshly. "Are you hoping to catch Shiner Crouse at some shady game, or what?"

"Could be. We'll have the answer to that, if and when," was Pat's terse response.

In less than an hour they drew near the shallow canyon into which Apache Crossing was tucked. The moon was near its zenith, throwing a pale clear light. From a quarter-mile away they learned the roadhouse was still holding high revelry, if the racket of the piano and the raucous voices meant anything.

"What makes you think Crouse isn't long gone from a place like this, Ezra?" Lanark challenged uneasily.

Ez didn't bother to answer. This time there was no attempt to cache the horses in safe cover. Stevens made for the notorious saloon and pulled up directly before the door. Careless of who might see them, they tethered the ponies to the rickety rail, ducked under and made for the door.

Only a momentary pause broke the uproar as they entered. Stevens was grimly pleased to see Lieutenant Crouse leaning indolently against the bar. Although somewhat altered in appearance by his civilian clothes, he had not shed his arrogant assurance. Downing the drink he held in his hand, he turned toward them swaggering. He was not drunk, but liquor had blunted any native caution he might have had.

"Well, Stevens! Checking on me, are you? Now you've found me, what about it?" he tossed out insolently.

Halting in the middle of the floor, Pat looked about carefully before answering. "Where did your friend get to, Crouse?" He was short. "I'd rather talk to him—"

The other's eyes widened. "Watching me that close, are you? Who says I've got any—friends, here or elsewhere?" he blustered.

Pat did not bother to spar. "There must be a dozen rooms in this place," he told the watchful Bar ES partners. "See what you can find. And you, Lanark . . . get outside there and circle the place before Grimes lights a shuck."

If the bartender made an ineffectual protest, Russ Crouse only lolled against the bar and laughed tauntingly. "That's right. This is off-limits for service personnel, Lanark," he advised brazenly. "I hate to report finding you here—but I may have to do it yet! I'll have a word to say about your free-and-easy parole officer too—"

Ignoring him, Lanark and the partners followed directions. Pat remained where he was, examining the officer with cool disfavor. "What will you have to say about me, Crouse?" he rapped.

Russ's cocky grin turned into an uncertain scowl. "You'll hear it, mister," he snorted. "All in good time! . . . Misusing your parole authority—and interfering with officers. I'll make you look good!" he promised with sinister irony.

"Don't waste your time," Pat said curtly. "If I'm forced to smash you, Crouse, I won't hesitate a second!"

Unimpressed, the man would have hurled more threats, but Ez came back into the bar, closely followed by Sam. "No dice, Stevens." The lanky redhead spread his big hands. "Shall we kick this fork-tailed puppy till talk rattles out of him—?" He indicated Crouse contemptuously.

Pat waved this proposal away, well aware that with a man of Crouse's caliber it would never work. He turned toward the door as Lanark appeared with a brief head-shake. He had found nothing.

Russ had been waiting for this moment. "Well, well." His sarcasm was blistering. "I don't know what you're trying to pin on me, Stevens! Won't it work?"

Pat paid no heed, motioning the others back when Crouse started boldly for the door.

"Too bad, Lanark," the latter called back from the opening. "For all you know I'm here on special assignment. But—you're—not!" With a sardonic chuckle he stepped out and was gone.

Moving slowly to the bar, the four men had their drink and stood there in gloomy silence. While they felt confident of laying hands on Cade Grimes at will, it was not the same thing as tying him to this rendezvous with Crouse. Pat shook his head slowly.

"You sure you looked this trap over real good?" he muttered.

Sam ducked an earnest nod. "We sure did. The store too—right to the cracker barrel."

Pat spun his glass away, straightening. "There's one slim chance left. We'll take a better look around outside."

The bartender and a slim handful of grizzled range men watched their movements warily without offering interference. Owlhoots occasionally took over Apache Crossing, brooking no obstruction of their will. As a consequence all strangers were accorded considerable respect here until their ultimate intentions became known. The behavior of Pat's party had bolstered the suspicion that they were fully capable of far rougher tactics.

Turning with one accord the four moved purposefully toward the door, and no hand was raised to stop them. In fact, the increase of the tired gaiety in the barroom as they stepped out said that a certain amount of relief was felt at their going.

The waning moon was still bright enough to lay a contrasting pattern of silvery light and black shadows over the canyon, etching the outlines of the roadhouse and the blunt pinnacles of jagged rock along the walls. Lieutenant Crouse had disappeared together with one of the horses at the rail. A faint clatter of gravel and stones came from some distance up the slanting trail. Ez listened to this keenly, then grunted. "One horse, Stevens," he growled. "Crouse is alone."

Pat verified this and dismissed it. "Circle the place," he instructed. "Watch for the least movement. We'll cover those sheds out back too while we're about it."

They set off, probing the deceptive shadows methodically, though scarcely expecting any practical result. If Cade Grimes had fled into hiding at the last minute, he certainly did not appear to be awaiting discovery here.

Lanark moved out to poke around an abandoned hog pen in the brush, and Sam circled a rotting woodpile and headed for a tool lean-to against the empty, sagging wagon shed. If they found nothing it was not for lack of diligence.

Ezra walked completely around a weathered grain bin, and stepped to the door. For a second the fact that the rusty door hasp was closed prompted him to turn away. Abruptly then, he unhooked the creaking door, flung it back and started in. An instant flurry of action ensued. Glancing that way, Pat saw a tangle of arms and legs roll out the door and resolve into two struggling men tumbling about on the hard-baked ground to the sounds of panting curses and an angry roar. He ran that way.

But Ez already had the situation under control, surging to his feet and hauling up a squirming captive. Pat was in time to wrench a waving six-gun from the man's grasp, and Ez straightened him up with a bony knee in his back.

"My, my. You really go for peace and quiet out here by yourself, don't you, Grimes?" Pat asked gently.

Cade sputtered his helpless rage. "Whyn't you birds leave me alone? . . . Lemme go! I ain't doin' nothing."

"It's what you've already done," Pat informed him with calm insistence. "What *was* the lieutenant paying you for tonight, Grimes?"

"It's a lie! Crouse didn't pay me for nothing. . . . I already told yuh all I know, Stevens!" Cade blurted vehemently. From the way he averted his desperate gaze, he was urgently wishing he had never seen these men.

Struggle was useless as Sam stepped forward and quickly went through his pockets. Ez only gripped him tighter. Sloan came up with a wad of greasy bills and stepped back. "Hundred and ten . . . hundred and thirty . . . hundred and fifty. Wow! If Crouse didn't pay yuh off, mister, then yuh don't need this!"

Grimes panted, sweating. "That's mine!" he croaked. "I earned it! . . . I—he did—that is—" He broke off, fully aware that he had given himself away.

"Oh. He *did,* then, eh? . . . What for, Grimes?" Pat demanded. "I wouldn't have said your services were that valuable—unless it was something special!"

When Cade hesitated Ez gave his pinioned arms a wrench. *"Ow!* . . . It was for—turnin' them roan strays back, Stevens!" His breathing rasped heavily. "I was only followin' orders! Crouse swore they'd be turned over to the Army in a few days—and they got 'em now, ain't they?"

Pat received this in dour silence. "You took them from that abandoned ranch on the bench too, didn't you?" he asked finally. "With the help of some Indian. And drove them to Crispel's Anchor, where you work—and where you know your way around!"

Once more the pain of his arms persuaded Grimes to confess. "Told yuh it was orders, didn't I?" he roared. "Crouse himself picked 'em up with an Army detail—"

"So he did. And I'm wondering why," returned Pat dryly. "Would you know if it was so he could put pressure on the Indian agent when he wanted to, Grimes?" he bored in.

Cade was reduced to simple panic by this time. He found something uncanny in this tall, cold-faced man's penetration. "I don't know," he gasped. "Lemme go, Stevens! My God, why don't yuh tackle Crouse himself with this stuff? I'm just a workin' puncher—"

Pat dropped his inquisition abruptly and stepped back. "Turn him loose, Ez," he ordered. After his pitiful tale of wholesale treachery for a price there was small hope of extracting more from this man.

Grimes staggered at his abrupt release, breathing noisily, and tenderly flexing his numb arms. "What'll yuh do with me now?" he mumbled apprehensively.

Sam tossed the dirty bills at his feet. "We don't want any part of you, scum," he rasped. "Get gone. Make tracks. Crawl back to your mudhole—"

Realizing his incredible luck at last, Grimes showed an astonishment in which lurked a deeper fright than before. "Yuh mean—" His quivering jaw snapped shut. Grabbing up the money, he scuttled away on hobbling boot heels.

Sam stared at Pat in the heavy silence which followed. "That was a put-up game, Stevens," he accused flatly. "Then yuh don't believe at all in this 'Indian ring' Haskins was squawkin' about—?"

"Who knows?" countered Pat evenly. "I'm following where the trail leads, Sam, and you can do the same. Or can you?" He grinned suddenly, turning away. "Let's clear out of this."

Reaching their mounts, they swung into the saddle. The roadhouse had fallen silent at last, and there was no other sign of life as they headed out of the canyon.

"Where now?" asked Lanark as the horses plodded up the trail to the plains level.

"We ought to be in time for breakfast in town," Pat returned easily. "I want to shove on to the fort this morning—just in case our friend Crouse gets ambitious."

Having watched Pat's handling of the brassy lieutenant a time or two, young Flint's attitude toward Crouse was undergoing a subtle change. "If he's smart he'll keep his mouth shut about us," he announced doggedly.

"Whatever gave you the idea he's smart?" Pat smiled. "Crouse is cunning, I'll grant. So is a wolf."

Reaching the desert, they headed for town at a leisurely pace. The moon sank as they rode and darkness returned, only to yield presently to gray dawn.

They had breakfast at the only restaurant the Agency afforded, waiting while the grumpy cook made coffee and fried their steaks. Emerging later on the street they spotted

Crispel, the self-assured agent, standing in his shirtsleeves at the door of Gundel's warehouse.

"There's your chance, Stevens," urged Sloan. "He'll be interested to know about Grimes—*and* his pal Crouse."

But Pat was not interested. "Crispel can take care of himself. I hope. He always has. . . . Let's get on over to the fort, shall we?"

The Army post was cheerfully bustling this morning when they rode up to the sutler's store. Lanark watched the troopers moving about their routine affairs with leaden eyes. Lounging about without haste, the four presently ran into Rafe Baker, the scout.

"Back again, Sloan?" Baker looked them over keenly. "Or is there somethin' on your minds?"

Pat nodded. "It's Crouse we're interested in, Baker," he said frankly. "I suppose he's on the post today—?"

Rafe shrugged. "Why not tackle his orderly?" he suggested. "He knows Crouse's business better than Russ does."

Pat looked interested. "Could we arrange a private word with him, maybe?" he queried. "Who is it?"

"Sergeant Shreeve." Baker told him where the orderly could probably be found. "Just make sure Crouse don't run into yuh. Nobody else cares."

Thanking the other, Pat headed across the parade, followed by his friends. Cavalrymen and civilian employees moved about the post, and their own activity was not particularly noted. At a corner of the officers' tack room Pat paused. "Wait here," he said.

A handful of orderlies were busy in the place when Pat entered. "Sergeant Shreeve?" he asked the first man he met. A thumb was jerked toward a grizzled, flat-faced non-com in one corner of the tack room. Pat walked over.

"Howdy. Are you Shreeve?"

The sergeant nodded alertly, cocking a crinkled eye upward. His gaze sharpened when Pat introduced himself as a friend of Flint Lanark. There was no missing the watchful glance he shot about the place. He knew what was coming.

"You're Lanark's parole officer, ain't yuh?" he brought out swiftly. "How is the boy—?"

"Okay. He's right outside now. Where is Lieutenant Crouse, Shreeve?"

The sergeant looked at him even more carefully, lowering his voice. "Who sent yuh—?"

"Rafe Baker," Pat said, and left it there.

"Then lay off," Shreeve warned cautiously. "I ain't paid to lie. Shiner Crouse is a rat, Stevens—but he's too smart to trip," he said bluntly. "I know what he's up to. I'm the only one, unless you're wise!"

Pat shook his head. "I don't get it. Who *is* Crouse, anyhow? VanOsdell's nephew?"

"Nothing like that." Shreeve waved a bony hand. "But he is a hold-over from our previous C.O. if that tells yuh anything. He practically runs the post for VanOsdell— and he has a finger in practically every department. That's a combination," he commented tersely, "that's kinda hard to beat."

Pat grew even more interested. He was confirming much now that he had long suspected. "And I suppose he lends a hand to the adjutant now and again too?" he suggested.

Shreeve looked surprised, but he nodded. "Sure he does," was the answer.

Pat thought it over swiftly. He was pretty sure he had what he needed. "Thanks, Sergeant. Crouse handles most of the post's dealings with the Indian Department, I expect—"

"If yuh mean has he got Crispel in his pocket—yes," growled the orderly sourly. "Don't yuh never tell where yuh got all this though, Stevens. And yuh better get out of here pronto," he advised pointedly.

Pat looked across at him shrewdly. "Russ likes to take it out on anybody who gets in his way. Is that it?"

Shreeve snorted. "Lanark's only a gnat for Crouse to swallow," he declared forcibly. "Or me either, for that matter!" His bitterness testified to past experience.

"It's cut and slash in all directions, eh?" urged Pat softly.

The sergeant's leathery face corded with resentment. "Did yuh ever try playin' rich, mister—able to grab anything yuh wanted? . . . The man don't know what it is to be told no!" he said harshly. For him that was Crouse's story in a nutshell.

It jibed with Pat's emerging picture of the overbearing officer. He was about to press the inquiry further when he heard a burst of louder talk from beyond the open window. He recognized Sam's voice, a note of warning in it.

"Much obliged, Sergeant. See you later." Turning away abruptly, Pat started toward the door. He barely made it, stepping into the open, when a man in the act of entering stepped quickly aside to avoid a collision. He was in officer's uniform, and Stevens found himself meeting Russ Crouse's level stare.

"After you, Stevens," the latter said sarcastically. "You're always welcome here. Snoop around as much as you please!"

It told Pat the man knew precisely what he had been about. Unfortunately for him, Crouse had been too late to prevent its accomplishment.

13

PAT EXAMINED him with hoisted brows. "Don't exaggerate your importance, Lieutenant," he murmured calmly.

It was the best answer he could have found. Jabbed briefly off balance, Crouse scowled. He tightened up fast. "I won't have to with you around," he retorted. "Considering where we last met, Stevens—and your visit to my orderly—we'll just put two and two together and come up with an answer you won't like!"

It was pure bluff, but Pat contrived to look startled as he glanced toward the tack room. "Did I miss—?" he began.

Crouse was laughing nastily. "You won't for long," he promised. "Word has come through that Adjutant Widmark will be here very soon, probably tomorrow. As it happens," he raised his voice for the benefit of Lanark who was listening twenty feet away, "I'm in a position to know what he'll say!"

"I'll remember you said that. The Colonel will be interested—since the only place you could learn is in those missing records."

Pat's flat statement sobered the vindictive officer in a flash. Russ looked daggers at him, and his savage fury could be detected under the well-controlled surface. "You talk a lot, Stevens!" he bit off tensely. "Just remember as parole officer to have your man available on demand!" With a snap of his heels on this parting shot he whirled and disappeared through the door.

Flint's face was white as they turned away. "He as much as promised me a conviction, Stevens!" he exclaimed harshly. "I haven't got a chance. . . . I'll break parole and pull out of the country—"

"No, don't try that," Pat contradicted quickly. "Crouse stands to lose more than you do, Lanark, whether you think so or not. Naturally he'll run a mighty stiff bluff. . . . Wait," he counseled. "Tough it out another day or so and I predict somebody else will crack first. Can you promise me that?"

Lanark would not promise, but he was submissive when Pat said they might as well pull out. They got their broncs and headed for the Bar H, where they arrived shortly before midday. Haskins was out somewhere on the range. But although Libby showed curiosity as to where Stevens had gone, she ignored Flint completely. Lanark shrank visibly at the slight, and shortly thereafter Pat found him saddling up once more.

"Where to now?" the latter asked pointedly.

Lanark was stern. "I ain't wanted here, that's sure. I'll see if I can help old Joe out—"

"Oh, come on now. Stick around. This can't last too much longer. I mean it."

Flint shrugged. "Haskins can't be far off," he muttered evasively. He swung up and reined away.

"Don't forget I'm trusting you, boy," Pat called after him. He made no further attempt to detain the trooper, and Flint soon faded from sight up the canyon.

The afternoon dragged by. Shortly before supper time the elderly rancher jogged into the yard alone. He looked up startled when Sam Sloan yelled at him, "Where's Lanark? Didn't he come back with yuh, Haskins?"

Joe shook his head. "Ain't seen him at all." His bushy white brows rose. "Don't tell me that boy ran—"

"No, no," Pat cut in firmly. "Naturally Lanark's upset. We learned that Army adjutant is due back soon. . . . Flint's gone off by himself to think it over," he concluded firmly. "He'll be back."

Ez looked at him with slow incredulity. "Hope you're right."

Not till the meal commenced without Flint putting in an appearance did Libby show any interest. Although she said nothing she glanced out into the yard with a preoccupied air. Pat let her fret, watching her secret uneasiness build up. The meal ended, and still Lanark did not show himself.

In spite of his assurance earlier, Stevens shared something of the girl's concern as darkness fell. He had not forgotten Flint's threat to desert and pull out. Heavy pressure had been brought to bear on him for a long time now, and it was growing no lighter. The cavalryman's distrust of officers was such that he may even have doubted Widmark's support in the face of court-martial proceedings.

"Sam and me'll take a *pasear* around, Stevens, if it'll do any good," Ez offered, noting his friend's uneasiness.

Pat shook his head. "You can't track before morning— if then," he pointed out. "If Lanark doesn't want us to follow his sign, he'll make sure we can't. And if he's coming back at all he'll come by himself."

"Why don't he, then?" Ez snorted. "The young fool ought t' be kicked!"

Pat was not to be provoked into discussion; moreover,

he avoided an obvious overture from Libby Haskins before turning in. He could only censure her under the circumstances, for she had helped to bring this situation on.

Morning dawned following an eventless night. Pat rose early, yet he was not ahead of Libby. She looked at him, sadly accusing, as he passed through the kitchen. "Something has happened, to make Flint disappear this way," she brought out with an effort.

For just an instant he remembered the Apaches. Was it barely possible that marauding raiders had caught Lanark off the ranch and wiped him out? Then Pat pushed this thought aside. Without saying anything he shrugged and moved on toward the door and into the yard. One of the partners began to stir about overhead as Pat entered the barn. Sam thrust his head over the edge of the mow, peering down owlishly.

"Oh. You, Stevens—?"

"Is Lanark up there?"

"You mean, did he show up durin' the night—?" Sam shook his tousled head. "No sign of him, boy."

Pat waited till he and Ez came down the ladder, and all three washed up outside the kitchen door. The old rawhides were aware from his set expression that Pat was thinking deeply.

"What now?" asked Ez gruffly.

Pat shook his head. "I don't know. He *may*'ve got a hunch of some kind and set off to investigate—" From his tone he did not even believe it himself. "I'll shove on into town this morning and look around."

Sam nodded sympathetically. "We'll come along."

"No, I want somebody here in case he shows up. I'll be back before noon. We'll just have to hope the Army doesn't show up before he does."

Breakfast was a silent and constrained affair. Pat shoved off soon afterward, and he made good time. It was ration day at the Agency, with scores of dark-faced Indians waiting stolidly about the building. Many Navajo families were temporarily camped nearby, their trim pinto ponies and brilliant blankets making a colorful display.

Pat observed at once, however, that something far more important than the supplying of Government wards appeared to be going on at the Agency. Some two dozen men stood on the broad porch, conversing absorbedly. Military buttons glinted amidst the drab range garb, and he saw Sheriff Lybolt among the others. Obviously some engrossing topic held their gravest attention.

There was no sign of Flint Lanark anywhere about, and Pat's first lively apprehension quickly subsided. *"He* can't have done anything to stir folks up this way," he mused.

Wary of calling attention to himself, he rode on down to the saloon. A gathering of freighters and roustabouts were busily discussing some recent event. He caught references to a smashed Army ambulance and to military details even now scouring the desert. Perhaps the anticipated raid by renegade Apaches had struck at last.

Buying a drink he didn't need, Pat leaned across the bar confidently, thumbing toward the talkers. "What's the pitch, bartender? I just got in—"

The man looked at him vaguely. "Been a double killing three or four hours below here on the Texas trail," was the startling answer. "Some Army bigwig got knocked off—can't say I remember his name. He was headin' here." He shook his head sagely. "Be hell to pay now!" He looked at Pat again quickly. "Which way did you say you came from—?"

Smothering a smile, Pat thumbed into the north. "I'm staying at Bar H with old Joe Haskins." Even as he spoke his thoughts were busy. There was no possible question but that the victim was Adjutant Widmark. At this news he decided he could use his drink after all. The bartender was called away but Pat started to talk to his neighbor at the bar and soon elicited such details as had been made public.

"No question about this being a murder, I suppose?" he asked, frowning.

"With a slug through both Widmark *and* the driver?" His informant scoffed. "Probably the killer tried to make it look like Apache work. They say that ambulance was deliberately stampeded into a wash, with the horses in a snarl! . . . A grudge killin', pure and simple!"

"When did this happen?"

"Sometime durin' the night. The news ain't an hour old—" The man's voice dropped. "There's a story that Jobe Fenner, the driver, wasn't dead yet—and if he comes to he'll talk." He paused, leaving it there. "Probably just a story."

Pretending to see someone he knew outside the door, Stevens quickly excused himself. Reaching his horse he jogged on down the street away from the Agency. Once he was beyond the edge of town he set off at top speed for the Bar H. His face was bleak when he rode into the ranch. Sam and Ezra were waiting, and Libby came hurrying from the house, no longer concealing her anxiety.

"Did you find him, Pat—?"

It answered the question of whether Lanark had returned of his own accord. Pat's look was reply enough.

"What *did* yuh learn there at the Agency?" demanded Sam shrewdly.

"It's Widmark. He and his driver were murdered on the trail last night, and the ambulance was wrecked."

Libby stifled an exclamation. "Oh . . . Pat! Surely you don't think—" Her hands went to her mouth.

"Hold on now. I don't think anything. And if any of you get Lanark mixed up with this thing in your minds, forget it."

"But—"

"No." Pat cut the protest off determinedly. "Easy does it. I know how bad things look. But we just—don't—know. I refuse to believe a thing till I'm sure."

Haskins showed up at that moment, and after one look at their faces, he had to be told the full story. Aware the young cavalryman had been missing for nearly twenty-four hours, he growled in his throat. "Humph! If Flint did that, he's smarter'n I thought," he declared cynically.

"*Dad!*" cried Libby. "You know Flint Lanark better than that—!"

"Well." Old Joe was grumpy. "Maybe I do. . . . Where *was* he then, girl?" he queried pointedly.

Her inability to answer filled her with dismay. Libby had recalled fully now her recent shabby treatment of the young fellow. "He—he'll explain when he comes back," she said, trying bravely to bolster her wavering faith. "He couldn't have done this to Mr. Stevens now, when he owes his very liberty to him!"

"Then he better be gettin' back fast," observed Ezra tonelessly. He was gazing off across the desert so fixedly that it caught the attention of the others. Looking that way, Sam made no effort to suppress a groan. "By gorry! Here comes the Army now," he announced tightly.

Pat saw that he was right. A detail of four men, closely grouped, was riding toward them, the blue of their uniforms a spot of color in the drab, brush-matted expanse of desert. An enormous silence gripped the onlookers as the advancing detail slowly grew in size and drew near, the sun glinting on ominously pommeled carbines.

Lieutenant Crouse rode in the lead. He made a dashing figure in tilted campaign hat and fringed gauntlets, with holstered dragoon Colts on his saddle. Sweeping into the yard with the trio of armed troopers deploying close behind, he hauled up with a flourish.

"Stevens, I've come to relieve you of your charge." He was being official, his parade-ground tone mockingly formal. "You will kindly produce Trooper Lanark at once."

Although well aware the other had instantly noted Flint's absence, Pat chose to equivocate mildly. "We couldn't know you were going to be here just at this time, Lieutenant," he said. "Lanark is out on the range—"

From Old Haskins' smug expression and Libby's poorly dissembled agitation, Crouse read the answer. He shook his trimly cropped head, looking grave. "Afraid I can't swallow that," he gave back coolly. "Luckily I suspected something of the kind and brought a detail along." He swung about lithely in the saddle. "Corporal! Take your men and search the ranch."

The non-com saluted smartly, rattling off an order to the two troopers. Dismounting, the three made quickly for the house and out-buildings.

"Lieutenant, this is pure foolishness!" Libby was both

scandalized and indignant. "Are you accusing us of lying or deception—or both?"

Crouse touched his hat to her, a sardonic gesture. "It was Stevens who spoke, I believe," he observed meaningfully. "I needn't remind you that Trooper Lanark's failure to appear on demand is a serious offense against regulations."

"What is it you want of Flint?" she demanded.

The officer showed a reluctant tolerance. "If Trooper Lanark is either arrested in hiding—or picked up in flight, as he surely will be—he'll be charged with desertion *and* murder," he predicted in clipped tones.

Pat listened stonily, not needing to be told that the officer was playing his authority to the hilt. "Easy, Crouse. Or you'll be called to account by a military court for prejudicing witnesses in this case—if there is a case," he warned thinly.

"Nonsense, Stevens." Russ was as smooth as polished steel. "The man's already formally charged with stock theft. Now the chief witness against him has been murdered—and Lanark isn't anywhere to be found. I leave it to you what construction a military court will place on those facts!"

His case appeared so watertight that his hardy air of assurance was nothing short of bragging. Hating the authority he represented, Joe Haskins glowered at Crouse bitterly.

"Yuh ain't proved a thing on that boy yet," he barked defiantly. "You're buildin' mighty high with bricks that ain't yet been made, mister!"

Crouse afforded the elderly rancher a venomous glance. "It would seem that Lanark is building his own scaffold," he retorted blandly. "I'll be obliged to report this suspicious disappearance—and whatever efforts are required for his recapture."

A sinister atmosphere hung over the ranch yard as the three troopers reappeared, tersely reporting failure to locate any sign of the missing man. It seemed futile to play for more time, but Stevens had to try.

"With Adjutant Widmark unavailable for testimony—

and those records missing—what exactly can be proved against Lanark?"

Crouse permitted a freezing smile to flicker briefly across his mouth. "Doubtless that's exactly the way Lanark himself figures," he retorted vindictively. "Unfortunately it's too late for him, or others involved, to dodge altogether. In fact, since nothing has been proved to the contrary, Haskins himself is quite likely to be charged with complicity in the theft of those horses. . . . I'll do what I can for him, of course." He shamelessly attempted to curry favor with Libby, at the same time congratulating himself that he had thrown terror into her crabbed and potentially troublesome parent.

Pat was ready for him. "I'd go slow with that stuff if I were you," he advised dryly, "before Haskins comes up with a surprise witness or two of his own!"

Crouse was in no mood to back down. His willingness to hurl threats, while his obvious duty waited, was proof in full of his malign purpose. "Oh—as for you, Stevens," he bit off, "your utter failure as a responsible parole officer will spell at least a jail term, I can promise you that!"

The words were scarcely out before hoofs clattered at the corner of the ranch house and Flint Lanark jogged into view. He hauled up short at sight of the Army detail. "Who's promising who?" he demanded. "I suspect I'm involved in this somewhere—and I want to know what's being said!"

14

A TENSE SILENCE existed for ten seconds as Crouse examined Flint with cold eyes. "Attention, trooper!" he barked finally. "Give an account of your movements for the past eighteen hours."

Lanark stiffened up instinctively, but his incredulous

stare was decidedly unmilitary. He was in no haste to make his response. "I was asleep for six and—working for twelve, sir," he declared grudgingly. "What business is that of yours—?"

The bold question was a sharp reminder of realities. Pat spoke up hastily. "You couldn't know that I brought back news of serious trouble from the Agency, Lanark," he began. "It seems that—"

"All right, Stevens," the officer cut in heavily. "Never mind the play-acting. I daresay it's no news to Lanark that Adjutant Widmark has been murdered. . . . Trooper," he flung wickedly at Flint, "your parole has been revoked and I'm taking you in custody now!"

Had Lanark suddenly been lashed across the face he could not have been more taken aback. *"What—?"* His keen tan face went a ghastly white. To anyone not deliberately obtuse, his amazement and dismay were unquestionably genuine. "Widmark *killed?* . . . You—you're not—" Suddenly he whirled to face Pat. "Stevens, is he lying again?" he blurted out.

The faces of his friends gave him the full answer. Crouse permitted no time for further protest. "Silence!" he roared, his face tightening with iron resolve. "Corporal, take this man in charge!"

Resenting their work and woodenly showing it, the three troopers slowly moved in Lanark's direction.

It is doubtful if Flint would have dreamed of resisting anyone but Crouse himself. The sudden disastrous news, however, triggered a violent reaction.

"Not by a damned sight!" he exclaimed. Clapping spurs to his alarmed pony he whirled the animal and broke away in full flight.

"Grab him, men!" Crouse cried instantly. "Shoot down that horse if necessary—!"

He knew it was not a government-owned animal. Pat read in a flash the man's purpose to make it look as bad for Lanark as possible. It was soon demonstrated that no such course was vitally necessary. The three troopers, old-line cavalry hands with hard-earned savvy, had read the condition of Lanark's mount.

In a burst of speed they swept after the fugitive, over-taking Flint with ease and closing in on both sides. Their strong distaste for this job was no bar to carrying out orders diligently and with dispatch. The grizzled corporal lunged out to grab Lanark's bridle rein. With an exclamation of despair Flint swung a fist at him.

The four horses slammed together, rearing and milling. Rising in his stirrups, a trooper dived at Flint from the other side. His arms closed about Lanark's waist. Both were torn out of the saddle and fell heavily to the dirt as the broncs danced apart. Hauled to his feet, Lanark gave up at once. Well aware of the hopelessness of his attempt, he slipped back into the silent obedience of the disciplined soldier.

"Secure his arms," Crouse ordered stridently, jogging out toward them. "This has gone far enough already! . . . Your conduct," he snapped at the granite-faced captive, "only goes to bear out my original charge of desertion! You'll be dealt with in short order by the proper authorities!"

When Lanark displayed no reaction whatever, Russ waved to the stony-eyed troopers. "On your way, Corporal! Conduct the prisoner to Fort McDonald, and deliver him at once to the guardhouse."

"Lieutenant!" called Libby, as the troopers turned away with Lanark in their midst. "Come here a moment, please—"

Crouse turned uncertainly, then rode toward her with condescending lack of haste.

"Lieutenant," she spoke up firmly as he drew close. "I won't attempt to question your duty. But if you accuse Flint Lanark untruthfully, or attempt to persecute him in any manner, I do not wish to see you again—here or elsewhere. Is that understood?"

Crouse looked fixedly at her small resolute face, refusing to take her seriously. A tolerant smile touched his mouth if not his eyes. "That sounds remarkably like illegal pressure, Libby," he drawled with an air obviously meant to be captivating. "You can't mean that! Suppose you wait, before accusing *me* of exaggeration, h'm?"

Her face paled as she saw that he meant to put her off. "At need I shall wait till Flint is relieved of all these vile charges, however long it takes," she retorted evenly. "Good-by, Lieutenant!"

Chuckling moderately, Crouse touched his hatbrim. "It's not that bad, I trust," he deprecated confidently. Wheeling his mount before more could be said, he cantered briskly off to catch up with his detail.

The group in the ranch yard stood looking at one another blankly, still surprised by the speed with which all this had happened.

Sam shook his head dolefully. "That boy sure didn't play his hand smart," he made lugubrious comment. "He ain't helpin' himself a bit!"

"It looked bad—that break he made," conceded Pat soberly. "If he'd been here so we could tip him off beforehand, he'd have made a better showing. On the other hand—" A measure of practical cheer returned to his tone. "That Crouse wouldn't have much trouble making an angel look shabby. We can hardly blame Flint for him!"

They discussed the situation at length. It was difficult to discern a single ray of light for Lanark under the damning circumstances. But Pat had no remote intention of giving up.

"We've still got those horses to think about," he said decisively. "If Lanark is the key to them, we'll just go on twisting till it works. . . . I'll give things time to shake down a little," he concluded, "and tackle Colonel Van-Osdell about this later in the day."

Haskins snorted contemptuously. "What'll *he* have to offer?" Old Joe was utterly disillusioned about the fairness or leniency of Army brass, and it came out now. " 'In the Army things must take their course, even if a man more or less gets killed for it,' " he mimicked savagely. "That's what old Van'll be tellin' yuh, Stevens!"

Pat shrugged. "Possibly. I won't know till I ask. At least he's convinced me that he isn't prejudiced."

Haskins completely missed the double-edged significance of the last comment. There was more talk, but it got nowhere. Toward midafternoon Pat set off for town with Ezra and Sam. Excitement at the Agency had largely died out, they found; the Indians, having received their rations, had departed and the sunny street was quiet. Asking the partners to linger, picking up what information they might, Pat shoved on to the fort alone.

Sheriff Lybolt was coming out of the sutler's store when he arrived. "Thought you'd give up by this time, Stevens," he remarked. Clearly he had heard the latest news.

"You'd think different if it was your money at stake—or that spotless reputation of yours," retorted Pat.

Gif scowled swiftly. But whatever he was about to say, he thought better of it and strode away.

Again Pat was forced to wait in the adjutant's office of the administration building. But when VanOsdell's visitor left, the Colonel showed himself in the doorway. "Stevens?" he said dourly. "Come in here, man."

Pat complied, closing the door behind him and moving forward to the C.O.'s desk. VanOsdell, who had been working over a mass of papers, tapped his pince-nez against a thumb and stared up from under his craggy brows.

"What was this uproar at the Bar H when a detail arrived to pick up Trooper Lanark?" he demanded abruptly.

"Nonsense." Pat met his severe eye coolly. "Lanark was on parole to me, Colonel, and when your detail stated its errand I turned him over promptly."

"I was given strongly to understand that he attempted to escape," pressed the grizzled officer thinly.

"He may have panicked for a minute." Pat spread his hands. "That top-lofty lieutenant of yours threw Widmark's murder at his head. I don't like that, Colonel. It might well have scared a better man."

VanOsdell froze. "I don't countenance criticism of my staff, Stevens!"

"You countenance their damned foolishness then," Pat said bluntly. "I don't think it's any under-officer's place to bring military charges; and nothing a court-martial can find will change that."

The Colonel showed his fairness by assuming a dignified calm. "I appreciate your views," he said moderately. "I can't overlook the possibility that Lanark's knowledge of guilt made him lose his head." His pause was austere. "There's more or less direct evidence, Stevens, that Adjutant Widmark's murder was committed by Army personnel," he proceeded firmly. "Lanark's refusal to explain a long interval out of your sight is unquestionably a black mark against him."

Pat saw that Russ Crouse had lost no time in spilling all he knew of a damning nature. He clung to the hope that no one could prove Flint's whereabouts overnight until the trooper himself talked. "I can swear that Trooper Lanark was completely unarmed while on parole to me," he said simply.

VanOsdell waved this away. "Apparently the killer begged a ride with that ambulance," he explained. "Pony tracks were found behind it—shod, I might add. He seems to have done his work with the driver's weapon. An attempt was made to make it look like Apache work— but the marks of Army spurs were found at the scene. . . . I don't care to tell more." He broke off curtly.

"What about this driver of Widmark's—Fenner," Pat probed keenly. "Has he been able to talk?"

"I can't tell you, Stevens."

"Then you are bringing this wild charge against Lanark on circumstantial evidence?"

VanOsdell looked at him coldly. "Trooper Lanark will get his hearing in the morning," was his dry response. "Good day, sir."

Pat would have attempted to elicit more, but for the Commanding Officer's forbidding air of finality. "Thank you, Colonel." With a curt nod he turned and left.

Ezra and Sloan were waiting for him on the steps of Gundel's supply store, below the Agency. Despite inquiries they had been able to pick up no fresh information.

"Get any satisfaction at all about them roans?" Sam asked, after hearing what little there was to be told about Lanark.

Pat shook his head. "The whole business seems to hinge on this killing now," he said.

"Hang it, Stevens!" Ez was frankly impatient. "We been jockeyin' around here for a week and we're still right where we started!"

Pat cocked a quizzical eye at him. "Do you want to pull out and leave Lanark in this pickle?"

"Didn't say that—"

"Then say something sensible."

There was little enough to be said until the cavalryman was given a hearing and they had something definite to go on. They rode slowly back toward the Bar H.

"The question is, where *was* Lanark overnight?" Sam put his finger on the crux of the situation unerringly. "It's plain he don't trust Crouse no more than we do. But if he was just sneakin' around to keep tabs on that oily character, he sure picked a sweet time for it!"

"On the other hand, maybe it was just the right time," retorted Pat. The others looked at him alertly.

"What do yuh mean by that?"

"Somebody killed Widmark. And it must have been somebody who stood to gain plenty by it."

"Then how could Lanark?" argued Sam. "According to him, Widmark was his best witness on this horse deal."

Pat gazed at him admiringly. "Real quick on the trigger, you are!" he complimented dryly. "That's exactly why I'm satisfied he's innocent—"

Sam scratched his head, frowning. "I still don't see how you're goin' to fasten any such thing as that on Crouse," he protested dubiously.

"Give him time," returned Pat easily. "Ten to one he'll do that for us himself. These cocky birds are all alike."

The subject was dropped as they came in sight of the ranch. But if they thought it necessary to pacify Libby they were mistaken. After taking them all in with one severe glance, the girl turned away. Nor did she so much as mention either Lanark or Crouse for the rest of the evening.

The night passed quietly. Haskins had set the follow-

ing day for calf-branding; and after breakfast, seeing old
Joe and his daughter turn out, Pat and the partners
threw themselves into the work. Despite the best possible
care stock did not prosper on this desert range. Pat
shook his head over the gaunt flanks and bony frames of
the steers. Once again he recalled Flint Lanark's sympathy
for the problems of the stubborn rancher.

It proved to be a hard day, the more so because they
determined to finish up the calf-branding at once. If they
were all aware that Lanark's fate might be determined
today at Fort McDonald it was not mentioned. Late
afternoon found the work practically finished. Pat used
this as an excuse to take note of the plucky girl's weari-
ness.

"Chase along to the ranch, Libby," he urged. "We'll
be done in an hour. You can get supper and rest a bit."

"I will, Pat," she agreed with relief. After a word with
Haskins she turned away.

Done before sunset, they turned the last of the stock
out on the range and jogged slowly homeward. An excellent meal awaited them. All were so tired that there was
little talk, and Haskins headed almost at once for his bed.

At dusk Pat was in the barn looking for something.
Suddenly it came to him that someone was talking out in
the yard. It could not be Sam or Ez, for they had decided
to drift the Bar H stock farther up the canyon toward
better grass. Listening intently, Pat heard first Libby's
voice and then a man's reply. Shamelessly he tiptoed
to the barn door and peered out. As he half-expected,
Russ Crouse had arrived and, finding Libby seated on the
kitchen doorstep, was engaging her in talk.

"I followed orders, Lib," he heard the officer's urgent
plea. "Don't blame me if that stupid trooper calls a
murder charge down on his own head!"

"Not at all. You had nothing to do with it of course,"
she retorted.

"Listen, Lib," Crouse said, trying to appear masterful.
"Get me right. No soldier in his senses wants trouble in
the regiment! It only spells hard feelings and disgrace. . . .
I begged Lanark to tell the truth and get it over with," he

continued persuasively. "If he sneaked off overnight on a private errand, why doesn't he say what it was? *I* can't force him to use his head!"

"You attended the hearing, I suppose?" she asked distantly.

"I had to! . . . Hang it all." Crouse pretended vast impatience. "That fool deliberately defied the Colonel. Why throw away his only chance—unless he knew he had none?"

"You're telling me now that Flint is guilty," said Libby tightly.

"But I tell you he must be! When are you going to quit clinging to a crazy, impossible hope? I can't see why you ever bothered to interest yourself in that fellow, Libby! . . . They say women have a soft spot for renegades," he pursued tolerantly. "But let's be reasonable about this. Because Lanark is no good—can't you comprehend that? He's breaking his neck to cover his tracks. And finally it led to this!"

"To your determination to smash him, I believe you mean?" she retorted as coldly as before.

Pat saw that she was pulling no punches; but at the same time he read a troubled indecision in her very vehemence, if Crouse did not. "Oh hell!" The officer showed sharp disgust. "I see I'm wasting time on both of you—" He started to rein away.

"Russ—wait!" Springing up, Libby walked out to stand at his side, and for a moment their low-voiced talk was indistinguishable. Not liking this, Pat cleared his throat and stepped into the yard. Crouse heard him. Whatever his reason, he spurred his bronc and was away with a rush, leaving Libby to stand disconsolate in the thickening dusk.

15

"IT WAS hardly decent of you to eavesdrop, Mr. Stevens,"
the girl said chillingly as he walked forward.

Pat ignored her tone of condemnation. "I'm wondering if I gave him time to make any promises," he answered thinly. "Did he?"

Impressed by the urgency of his manner, Libby fal-
tered. "He—promised for my sake to urge Flint to
greater frankness," she admitted.

Pat grunted, unimpressed. "I suppose that means he'll
do his best to get Lanark to admit that murder and be
done with it!"

"But where *was* he, Pat? Why doesn't he tell?"

Stevens saw that the poison of creeping doubt, cunningly fostered by Crouse, was gnawing at her faith.
"Libby, I don't know. Evidently Lanark can't bring himself to say just yet. But that doesn't mean we need to let
him down."

"I know." She was clearly miserable. "But as Russ—
Lieutenant Crouse pointed out, he's steadily getting deeper
in the mire. . . . *Did* he sell those roans to us honestly,
Pat?"

Pat glanced at her sharply. "Said so, didn't he? And
Adjutant Widmark was on his way here to agree to that,"
he reminded.

"But—if Mr. Widmark had something else to say . . .
I mean," she pressed on hurriedly, "who else would wish
to silence him badly enough for murder?"

It struck Pat that the scheming Crouse had made an
even greater impression on her than he had supposed.
"You can't think of anyone, eh?" With this cool retort he
lapsed into silence. Sam and Ez came riding into the

yard at that moment, and after a brief show of uncertainty Libby turned to enter the house.

Pat joined the weary partners at the corral. While they were off-saddling he gave a terse account of Russ Crouse's visit. "Lanark's in a jam, and no mistake," he acknowledged. "From what I gathered, his hearing was in the nature of an indictment, and he's being held for court-martial."

"Yuh mean he ain't told VanOsdell yet where he was overnight?" Sam was incredulous. "He must be askin' for it, Stevens!"

Pat shook his head. "The way I figure it, Lanark is badly scared and he doesn't trust anyone—although he might listen to me." He pondered the matter, and presently spoke up once more. "Will you take a ride over to the fort in the morning for me, Sam?"

"What for?"

"Get hold of Rafe Baker. Ask him to get word to Lanark. He'll know how. Tell him to warn Flint that he's got to talk—at least to VanOsdell. He's just cutting his own throat with this silence. We've got to get that over to him somehow."

"What'll he tell the Colonel?" growled Sam, who thought the whole scheme was impractical.

"He's got to cover himself at least for the time of the murder. Be sure Baker makes him understand that somebody's after his hide and he's got to fight back."

"He ain't yet," Sam pointed out. "What if he won't?"

"Baker can tell him about Shiner Crouse spending his time out here," supplied Pat shrewdly. "Remind him he's just giving that yellowleg a better chance at his girl."

Ez nodded his head sagely. "That ought t' do it if anything will," he judged.

They talked it over a few minutes longer before turning in. Sloan was smart enough the following morning to appear to have nothing on his mind. He waited longer than usual for breakfast, chaffing Libby good-humoredly. But the girl was not to be jollied out of her listlessness. She fed the men and did not appear to notice as Sam saddled up and rode away.

He was gone for three hours, returning to find Pat waiting on the trail. "I ran Baker down and set him to work," he reported. "He thinks too that Lanark is foolish not to talk, and talk loud and fast."

"But you didn't wait for an answer?" asked Pat in a vexed tone.

Sam looked blank. "Shucks, no. Rafe'll have to pull strings to get word through to the guardhouse, Stevens!" he answered defensively. "No tellin' whether there'll be an answer—"

Pat shrugged. "Does Baker know when that court-martial is set for?" he asked keenly.

Sam said no. "The C.O.'ll have to call in other ranking officers, won't he? It'll take time to arrange, and I reckon we'll hear."

If Stevens had hoped the Army scout might send some word of encouragement out to the Bar H he was disappointed. He had forgotten to ask Sam to check on the confiscated roans that morning, but did not ask Ezra to make good the omission.

On the following morning, however, he rose purposefully from the breakfast table and announced his intention of riding in to the post for news. Ez and Sam said nothing about accompanying him. It was just as well Libby not be aware they had been told to maintain a watch for Russ Crouse and to keep him away from her if possible.

A mile from the Agency Stevens swung off to avoid the town, riding straight across the desert to the fort. He was yet some distance from the parade-ground when he became abruptly aware that something unusual was going on. A trumpet blasted musically, clear as a bell in the thin air. Cavalrymen ran here and there in the sandy barrack streets. Presently an armed detail was mustered and mounted their horses.

The first detail had barely got away when a second fell in. Curious at once, Pat drew rein at the edge of the parade to watch this. The thin bark of orders drifted to his alert ears. He saw now that several armed details were being hastily mounted and thrown into action, fan-

ning out from the fort in every direction. One cut across
the parade not far from his position, the early sun
glinting on their slanted carbines. The troopers looked
sober and intent.

A moment later he was approached from behind by a
foot guard. "Halt! Give an account of yourself, stranger—!"

"Stevens is the name, soldier. On my way in to see
your colonel," supplied Pat laconically, turning slowly
to face the sentry. "From here it looks like there was a
little excitement this morning," he proceeded with more
assurance than he felt. "Do you know what's up?"

The answer was a curt nod. "Prisoner escaped from
the guardhouse, Stevens. Afraid I'll have to turn you over
for questioning—"

Pat's laugh was a masterpiece of amused incredulity.
"I got here just this minute, soldier," he declared simply.
"Run your eye over my back trail there. . . . If *I* had
anything to do with a jail break," he chuckled ruefully,
"you certainly wouldn't be talking to me now!"

His very casualness carried conviction. The guard's
rigidly presented weapon slowly came down. "True for
you," he granted. "You don't look that foolish—" This
was accompanied by a hasty look about. "Just get where
you're goin', can't yez, so I needn't be explainin' my fool
head off."

"I'll do that." Pat nodded his thanks and set off for
the sutler's store.

Rafe Baker was leaning against the giant rear wheel of
a parked freight rig, his feet and arms crossed. He did not
move as Pat drew up nearby and dismounted, but the
warning look of his slitted eyes was plain. "Yuh picked an
awful bad time to show up here, Stevens," were his first
muttered words.

Pat's brows rose. "Lanark, was it?"

"As if you couldn't guess!" Baker jerked a grim nod.
"He's gone, clean as a whistle. Shows how much good it
did to get a message to *him*." There was irony in his
steady glance.

"You did what Sam asked, then?"

"Talked to him myself—"

"Did he tell you anything?"

"Not a thing." Baker looked faintly angry over this. "He listened—and I sure rammed it into him. But he wouldn't talk, at least to me!"

"He's young. Lord knows what's going through his head. If we had half the troubles he's got, Baker, we'd be careful of our own talk."

"Guess you're right," Baker said tersely. "I *was* able to tell Lanark his court-martial was scheduled for next month."

"Next *month?*"

Baker nodded. "I got it right away that he thought they were lettin' him rot in the guardhouse. It could be months before he comes to trial. . . . And if old Van is transferred in the meantime, that boy could be railroaded. He probably knows that."

"He may be anyway," Pat said. "And don't overlook that every day Lanark stays in quad makes Widmark's killer just that much safer."

"Yes—" The scout did not appear to find this statement surprising. His keen eyes narrowed. "Yuh weren't around here last night, were yuh, Stevens?" he asked abruptly.

Pat's starting smile froze. "Oh, for cripe's sake, Baker!" he protested. "You're not trying to tell me *I* had anything to do with this—?"

"Nope." The dry answer was unexpectedly prompt. "Just figurin' the way others will think," Rafe assured. "Jobe Fenner died last night—without namin' anybody. . . . Foolish as it sounds, Stevens, you better have your answers ready." He nodded up the street significantly.

Pat looked up to see Lieutenant Crouse bearing down on him with a guard in his wake. Russ's head was thrust forward and his eyes twin points of fire—he looked very much as if he were congratulating himself on this meeting.

"Fancy finding you here, mister," he opened up derisively, coming to a halt. "Rather inconvenient for you, I'll grant!"

Pat regarded him levelly. "Never mind the build-up, Lieutenant," he rapped. "Say what you've got to say."

Crouse's triumphant air was comment in full as he turned to address the guard. "Take this man in custody," he ordered brusquely. "The Colonel will like to hear his —excuse for still being around the fort this morning!"

Pat looked in disgust at the listening scout. "Tell the busy Officer of the Day I just got here, Baker," he suggested.

Crouse looked at him wide-eyed. He was enjoying this. "Would you vouch for this man, Mr. Baker?" he inquired mockingly.

Rafe shrugged. There was no alteration of his bored air, nor did he bother to speak.

"All right." Pat shrugged, turning toward the guard. "Let's get this over with. Baker's right that far."

Crouse would not permit himself to be deflated, leading the way officiously to the Adjutant's office. VanOsdell was there, conferring with staff officers. At length Crouse signaled that he was free. The guard herded Pat in to face the grizzled and preoccupied C.O.

"Well—well." VanOsdell peered over the tops of his glasses sharply. "You again, Stevens. What's this I hear about your prowling around the fort at the time Trooper Lanark escaped from the guardhouse?"

"I wouldn't know," drawled Pat. "Probably the worst construction possible to put on it. . . . In fact," he drove on, "I rode in this morning from the Bar H to make arrangements to see Lanark myself. A few words with Joe Haskins or his daughter will confirm that—"

The Colonel showed faint irritation. "It may not be your fault that Haskins and his family are also friends of Lanark's. In view of the fact, however," he said precisely, "I could hardly regard the testimony of either as final."

"That's a switch," Pat retorted. "Where the Army's concerned, everybody is considered guilty until proved innocent. Is that it?"

VanOsdell frowned on what he regarded as levity. "What is your opinion of the reason Lanark chose to go AWOL—if nothing worse, Stevens?" he queried.

If it was a loaded question Pat was ready for it. "I don't think the man's guilty of anything worse than nerves;

but I'll say frankly, I know nothing about his reasons. You've seen to that pretty thoroughly yourself——"

"Is that the reason you tried to get a message in to him?" put in VanOsdell unexpectedly.

Weighing this, Pat did not find that it constituted evidence of treachery on Baker's part. Possibly the scout had started a deploying rumor to cover his own tracks. "Am I to take it you recommended abandoning your friends altogether, Colonel?" Pat countered flatly.

VanOsdell's lined face was expressionless. "Still, it is strange you should show up the minute the prisoner made good his escape," he insisted.

"The truth *is* strange, in this case," conceded Pat. "But even in the Army I expect you've heard of coincidence——"

Moving to the Colonel's side, Crouse bent down to whisper something to him. VanOsdell frowned, shaking his head. But a fresh glint appeared in his eyes. "You seem to be treating this whole thing as a joke, Stevens," he challenged hardily.

"And I suppose that's the reason I'm spending weeks away from my own business." Sarcasm put an edge on Pat's terse response. "I'm not even talking to you right now of my own free will. . . . Let's get this straight, shall we? Half an hour ago I didn't even know Lanark wasn't in the guardhouse. I don't know if he slugged his guard, tunneled under the wall, or simply walked out. Now if there's anything else I can satisfy your curiosity about, sir, I'll be glad to oblige."

Once more Crouse started to whisper to his superior. Seeing this, Pat gave him no chance.

"After your remark on the subject, Colonel, I hesitate to criticize your——staff," he continued boldly. "But while you're listening to his advice, are you under the impression that Lieutenant Crouse is a disinterested party?"

Russ strove afresh to intercede. But VanOsdell impatiently waved him to silence. "What? What's that——?" he barked tartly.

Pat's nod was coolly self-possessed. "The Lieutenant is over quite often, talking to Haskins' daughter. He's taken her riding at least once—and I understand they enjoy each other's company at the post dances, although Trooper Lanark seems to consider her his girl. But this, of course, has nothing to do with the illegal sale of Army stock," he pursued almost casually.

The Colonel refrained from looking at Crouse, but his manner changed. It was almost as if he had made up his mind with some abruptness. "All right, Stevens. That's sufficient gossip," he said with distaste. "Is it clear that you're being released with the understanding that you'll be expected to work with us?"

"Just what would that mean, Colonel?"

"Nothing mysterious about it! If you see Lanark at any time, Stevens, it's your plain duty to turn him in to the proper authorities. I won't tolerate any other procedure, do you hear?"

Considering his tone of voice, it seemed safest to give assent. Five minutes later Pat was unhurriedly remounting his bronc. No one offered to prevent his departure, nor did Russ Crouse again put in an appearance. But heading back to the Bar H, Pat would have been the first to concede his growing depression.

"Libby hit it right," he reflected. "Lanark's every move only makes it look worse for him. Either Crouse has maneuvered him into a tight corner or Flint is as crooked as they come."

He had thought his problem through by the time he reached the ranch. Libby stood at the kitchen window, studying his face as he rode into the yard; she did not come to the door. Ez and Sam were waiting for him at the corral. His bleak face told the nature of his news.

"Good gravy! They ain't hung him, have they?" exclaimed Sam in mock alarm.

Pat shook his head without cracking a smile. "Looks like they won't for a while," he announced. "Lanark flew the coop last night. He broke out of the guardhouse, and nobody knows where he is—"

"Then he's out. So what's bad about that?" Sloan refused to take it seriously.

Pat shrugged. "At this rate you might as well kiss those roans goodby," he said plainly. "But it's not that I'm thinking of so much as—'' He broke off, gesturing mutely toward the house.

Ez got it. "We can't leave it this way," he agreed soberly. "So what'll we do, Stevens?"

Pat had his answer ready. "The only chance to save Lanark now is to get hold of him quick," he declared. "It's hopeless to try and track him from that guardhouse, I know. Do you think there's any chance of finding him, Ez?"

Scratching his head, the lanky tracker wouldn't say yes or no. "Yuh sure think up some tough ones,'' he grumbled. "This is the kind that takes some rollin' over. . . . I'll see what I can do." Press as they might for an expression of opinion, he would say no more.

16

THOUGH EZ would work diligently for Joe Haskins at dire need, they were so nearly two of a kind in gnarled independence that they were not good friends. Sam was therefore considerably surprised when, that evening, the tall redhead made a point of seeking out the rancher and starting a desultory conversation.

"What's *he* up to?" Sam muttered to Stevens as they watched this.

Pat's steel blue eyes crinkled in speculation. "No idea. Let's find out," was his practical response.

They drifted out to join the two in the ranch yard. Ez looked up at their arrival but did not break off his talk. He was playing cunningly on old Joe's natural sympathy for Flint Lanark.

"Lanark never asked for this grief, that's sure," Ez sourly ended a long diatribe. "Makes yuh wonder how come he ever wound up in the Army. Where is he from, Haskins?"

"Oh, he belongs in this country."

"He does?" Ez pretended surprise. "That's odd—"

"What's queer about it?" growled Joe.

"Why—he seems such a lone wolf, somehow. Ain't he got no family?"

Haskins shook his head. "No, yuh might call the boy an orphan, if he wasn't man grown." Noting the interest of his audience he continued. "Flint was born and raised on a small ranch over north here against the hills. His ma passed away when he was twelve or so. Abe Lanark had Injuns to contend with, same as me. He never prospered. Did all his own work and just sort of hung on."

"What about Flint? Didn't he help his old man?"

"Oh yes. Seemed like he was born on a horse. When his ma died, he turned to and helped work the range. Good as a man, he was. It made a man of him too."

"How come his pap ain't around now?" put in Sam.

"I'm comin' to that. Flint always was a silent boy. The more somethin' meant to him the quieter he'd be. It was three months before we learned Abe Lanark got killed by a fall from a horse! Flint buried him and just stayed there by himself. . . . That was a couple years ago this past season."

It was not unlike many another story of the lonely range country. Ez nodded his comprehension. "So Lanark got fed up with livin' alone and joined the Army?"

"He didn't have no choice," was the terse response. "Rustlers got his little bunch of cows. I never did hear whether it was that Three Rivers crowd or what. . . . Flint rode into Fort McDonald and joined up. We kind of figured it was because he aimed to stay near horses."

There was nothing here about Lanark's interest in his daughter Libby. The trio noticed the omission. "He'd ride out to see you folks once in a while, though?" Ez asked.

Old Joe agreed absently. "We always was neighbors. A man's got to have somebody. Flint knowed my Libby since they was kids. For a while there I thought he was interested in her. But I don't know." The leathery rancher frowned at some thought of his own.

"Did Lanark like the Army?" Pat put in curiously.

Haskins glanced up. "That's funny, too. I figured he did, Stevens. He got along well for a year or two. . . . Then lately he's been gettin' in trouble."

They discussed this briefly. But if Lieutenant Crouse had gone out of his way to plunge the cavalryman in difficulties, Haskins had not observed it. Pat nodded at this. It fitted in admirably with Russ Crouse's secretive methods.

"That old ranch of Lanark's," said Ez finally. "Gone to rack and ruin now, I expect. . . . Where is it, anyhow?"

"The Oasis?" Haskins shrugged. "It's been abandoned for months, of course. Never did get around to ridin' over there since Flint quit." He pointed out the direction.

Unsatisfied, Ez asked for further details, making sure he could find the place. Haskins described a few landmarks, and glanced at Ezra shrewdly. "Ain't aimin' to find anything over there, I hope?" he queried scornfully.

The answer was curt. "Don't know." Ez relaxed then. "Still, the place *is* a part of Lanark's story. Might look it over sometime if we're ever over that way."

The talk turned to other aspects of Lanark's predicament, and his little spread was not mentioned again. But on the following morning Ez routed out his friends at the crack of dawn. Sam was immediately interested.

'Takin' a whirl at trackin' Lanark today?" he asked as they washed up for breakfast.

Ez was uncommunicative. "We'll have a look at that Oasis outfit anyway. Might tell us somethin'."

Libby showed unmistakable signs of having spent a restless night. She said little, serving breakfast with her usual deft competence. Studying her, Pat guessed she was far from happy. Not even her father's critical comments on the coffee seemed to make an impression. After the meal Pat drew Haskins aside, gesturing back in the direction of the kitchen. "Be a little patient with her today," he suggested mildly. "She's a lot like Lanark—and having a hard time just now."

Old Joe snorted. "She'd be better off if she'd just stay

away from them Army lizards," he growled. Never a man to be fooled for a second, he was fully aware of his daughter's stubborn interest in the suave lieutenant from McDonald.

Pat read his thought. "That business may straighten out of its own accord," he predicted easily.

"If it don't, I'll straighten it out myself," threatened Haskins tartly. "It's got to me that the Army brass has been talkin' up an Apache outbreak. . . . Pah! Just a smoke screen to cover up their own runnin' around!"

"Nothing to it, eh?"

"Been five years since an Apache showed his face in this country." Haskins snorted again. "I've seen it all, Stevens! But do they come and ask me my opinion?"

Smiling, Pat turned away. Ez and Sam were waiting, having saddled his bronc for him. A few minutes later the trio were riding across the desert flats. Ez made no bones about heading straight for the little ranch called the Oasis.

They rode easily, stopping at a rock tank to refresh the horses. The sun blazed in a coppery sky by the time they drew near the tumbled mountain heights hemming in the desert on the south. Paying strict attention to the landmarks Joe Haskins had mentioned, Sam kept looking around. Finally he spoke.

"Same way we came on the way down," he announced. "I remember skirtin' that butte yonder—and if Haskins is right, Lanark's Oasis is right there on the edge of the hills." He pointed.

Pat nodded quickly. "And furthermore, we've seen the Oasis before," he seconded. "It's the place where we put those roan strays in the corral—"

"Hey—that's right." Ez was equally interested. "We just didn't know Lanark then, or if he owned a place. Cade Grimes knows this ranch too—and I reckon others."

The fact that they had already seen the old Lanark place did not induce them to turn back. Old Joe's story had fostered a keener interest in the site, and all were eager to look it over again.

The bold bench on which it was situated rose into view as they advanced. This time they rode forward without any attempt at concealment. A half-obliterated cattle trail wound up the slope at an easy grade. Finally their heads rose above the level of the bench and the log ranch cabin came into view, its slab door sagging open and the empty corrals beyond only adding to its air of blank desolation.

Drawing rein, they dismounted a rod or two from the house. Ez swept a single keen glance about. "Keep your eyes open for tracks," he ordered. They went over the place even more thoroughly than before. But except for old tracks of their own making and the sign left by Grimes which they had trailed to Crispel s Anchor, they found nothing.

Stepping out of the empty house without having detected evidences of recent occupancy, Sam shook his head. "Been a long time since Lanark's been back here," he hazarded.

Ez neither contradicted him nor made any immediate comment. "Might as well eat our bite here," he said finally. "There's water there in the corral trough today."

Pat turned to glance up at the sky. The stock tank had been dry on their last visit. But a storm had rumbled across the mountains yesterday, not reaching the desert. Perhaps the run-off in the canyons had once more filled the lower springs, setting them aflow.

They ate in the meager shade of the doorway, gazing out across the miles of empty flats to the flat-topped buttes and crumpled ranges beyond. It was easy to understand how a man could grow attached to such lonely spots.

The broncs, off-saddled and turned into the corral, were dozing peacefully. When they had finished eating Sam and Pat soberly discussed young Lanark's probable whereabouts without getting anywhere. Ez ignored the conversation, wandering about with restless curiosity. Later as the brassy sun shifted westward, he leaned his shoulders against the shaded end of the log cabin and closed his eyes. His even breathing soon told that he was taking forty.

"Don't bother him none whether Lanark headed for Montana or not," growled Sam disgustedly.

Pat smiled. "Let him rest. I asked Ez to try and find Lanark; and he's got his own way of going at a thing."

Sam snorted. "Goin' at it backwards, he is!"

Ez awoke an hour later, rising to his feet purposefully. "We ain't looked through these hills, Stevens," he announced needlessly. "Let's do that now."

Sam glanced up at the rugged slopes and glared at his partner contemptuously. "Ain't aimin' to find gold up there, are yuh?" he snapped, showing his scorn for the proposal.

Ez looked at him aloofly. "You stay here," he directed. "I don't want you to wear yourself out."

Sam displayed his willingness to be contrary, saddling up briskly and ostentatiously waiting for the others. They set off, winding up a narrow gully behind the bench, which gradually deepened to a canyon of impressive proportions.

They proceeded slowly, keeping a watch for anything of particular interest. At a distance of less than a mile from the abandoned ranch they reached a natural, grassy bowl in the sheltering hills, hedged about by cottonwoods and with a shallow stream meandering along one side. Pat looked it over appreciatively.

"This is why they called Lanark's place the Oasis," he guessed aloud. "Probably the house was originally built out there on the bench to guard against Indians."

They explored a few side canyons—some affording good graze but all empty and silent now—and were surprised on returning at last to the ranch to find it nearly sunset. The fact decided Sam. "Nothing here for us," he said conclusively. "If you're satisfied, Ez, we'll shove on back to the Bar H before we starve to death."

Still Ez made no cutting retort—a sure sign of his preoccupation. Glancing absently at Stevens, he shrugged. "Let's go—"

They left as they had come, making no effort at concealment. Gray dusk swam up out of the desert brush as they descended to the level. Even when the shadows grew thick Ez persisted in glancing back. "What now?" Sam snarled, out of patience with him.

Ez halted. "Nothin'. Only we're goin' back there again —and this time without showin' ourselves."

Pretending amazement, Sam argued vigorously. But the lanky tracker won. "You'll get your answer," he retorted to every incredulous question. Abruptly giving up, Sloan turned his horse. Even his grumbling died out at Ezra's sharp request for quiet, and they rode in silence.

Night had descended by the time they stole up the far end of the bench, dismounting and ground-anchoring the ponies near the top. They crept on toward the lonely ranch, straining their senses. It was Pat who first detected a faint sound of movement near the dark house.

"Psst!" He warned the others, who froze. Then Ez spotted a faint flicker of light. Someone was at the ranch.

"Spread out and close in," muttered Ez, not at all surprised. "And watch out for squalls—"

They separated, stealing around the cabin. After a delay Pat made straight for the shadowy door. Aware of his friends near at hand, he paused there, waiting. A faint scratch sounded inside—a match flared yellow. Peering cautiously in, Pat was genuinely startled.

"Howdy, Lanark," he brought out unguardedly, in a natural tone. "What in creation are you doing here—?"

The match died abruptly and boots rasped. "Stand away," came the tight order. "I got that door covered!"

Pat's laugh jarred. "Slack it off, man," he urged calmly. "Only Sam and Ez are with me. You're free as a bird, boy —we only want to talk."

Flint's delay said he was thinking fast. Finally he spoke. "Strike a match, Stevens," he growled. "And all three show yourselves—!"

Pat complied, deliberately avoiding hasty movements. Ez and Sam spoke, coming forward to the door. As they had suspected, Lanark was unarmed, and had been since his escape. Satisfied, he grudgingly lit a flare and turned. They exchanged a silent scrutiny.

"Well, Lanark! You seem to have landed yourself in a real jackpot now," Pat offered without emphasis.

Flint looked grim. "I suppose I am. I just couldn't take no more of it—"

Pat was easy with him. "You know Army discipline," he said simply. "Why didn't you talk?"

"What for?" Lanark glowered. "Who'd ever believe I come here often? The Colonel would just laugh!"

Pat did not agree, but he declined to argue. "So this is the answer, eh?"

Lanark nodded curtly. "The lead-pipe from the spring to the horse trough was busted, Stevens. I was fixin' that the evening Widmark got killed. I spent the night here. . . . Now ask me why I didn't tell Shiner Crouse that!" he burst out despairingly.

Ezra's nod was shrewd. "I noticed the pipe workin'. Knew somebody'd been around," he remarked.

"Sure. But how could I prove that? I didn't even expect you to listen, Stevens!"

Pat shook his head. "Better give yourself up, Lanark," he advised strongly. "You can't hide out here forever. Stand trial and clear your name," he urged. "We'll back you up, I can promise you that."

"You have all along," Flint acknowledged. "But it's no go. I'm being framed and railroaded, Stevens—right from Sheriff Lybolt on up to the Colonel himself! I tell you it's hopeless—"

"Don't say that," contradicted Pat firmly. "It's exactly what Crouse set out to make you think. . . . I tell you what," he broke off, demonstrating accurate knowledge of the other's state of mind. "Why not talk this over with Libby? She's changed her opinions considerably in the last couple of days—and she's levelheaded. Believe me, she lit into Crouse over his crooked capers! Maybe," he proceeded craftily, "she can help you see this thing straight, boy."

Lanark alerted briefly at the suggestion that Libby was no longer solidly in favor of Crouse. "I—" he began, then momentarily all but choked up. "I'll talk to her anyhow," he owned at length. "If she's willing—"

"She is. Get your bronc, Lanark, and we'll shove off. Nobody'll be looking for you at the Bar H, and we'll be there long before daylight."

Flint did not say where he had borrowed or commandeered his mount. It was a good one. He stole out into the dark and was back in three minutes, anxious now to follow out Pat's proposal.

They rode away swiftly. Even in pitch darkness Lanark's sense of direction was unerring, and the rising moon found them on familiar range. An hour after midnight they reined up in the Bar H yard.

The house was dark. "Wait, Stevens. I'll crawl in the hay and talk to her in the morning," Lanark urged, nervous now that the fateful interview loomed close.

"No, let's get it over with. Libby'll thank us." Pat started for the house. "I've got a hunch this talk will relieve her mind aplenty."

Flint subsided, waiting uneasily. Pat entered the ranch house, going directly to old Joe's room. The rancher was sleeping heavily. "Wha—what's that?" he sputtered when Stevens woke him. He sat up in bed slowly. "Libby, yuh say? Why, she's in her room, boy—"

"Go get her."

Haskins heaved out of bed, peering at him strangely in the lamplight. Then he plodded off in his flapping nightshirt. He was back in a trice, eyes blazing, his mouth gaping.

"My God, Stevens! What time is it?" he gasped. "I thought Libby was back from town hours ago, and sound asleep. But she ain't! Her room's empty, and she's clean disappeared!"

17

FOR REASONS of his own Russ Crouse had been willing to forego accompanying any of the several details dispatched in pursuit of Trooper Lanark. When a day passed and the details straggled into the fort empty-handed, Colonel VanOsdell called a staff meeting at headquarters to discuss the situation, considered grave because Lanark's successful escape appeared to put the solution of Adjutant Widmark's murder further away than ever.

The two post guides were present, and the meeting was brief but stormy. The C.O. was inclined to blame service negligence all around. "Come, come, gentlemen," he said angrily. "Surely some of you must have an idea where an AWOL trooper might be expected to go!"

None of the officers had anything to offer. Rafe Baker sat in a corner, chewing tobacco surreptitiously. He cleared his throat in the silence. "Might help to study young Lanark's ideas a mite," he offered laconically. "What's he after? . . . You know him as well as any, Crouse."

Russ was too fast on his feet to show confusion. "Don't confuse me with someone else," he retorted, a wicked edge to his carefully controlled voice. "I scarcely know the man! He belongs in G Troop."

Since he was himself in charge of A, this answer was aimed chiefly at the Colonel. Baker took it up.

"Wasn't you on loan to Lybolt when them roans was picked up?" he asked shrewdly. "You reported their loss. And I seen you dancin' with Lanark's girl at the last shindig—"

Crouse flushed hotly. "Doing my duty doesn't make me post nurse," he rasped, deeply displeased at all this attention. "And I'm not aware that our troopers are allowed—camp followers, either."

VanOsdell broke this up. "Bickering will not locate our man," he said severely. "Can anyone offer a practical suggestion?"

His tone silenced Baker. The meeting ended shortly thereafter, but animosities flared anew twenty minutes later, when Crouse ran into the sandy-haired scout crossing the hard-packed parade in back of officer's row.

"What's this idea you have in your head about me, Baker?" he challenged severely. He knew the scout to be both deep and crafty, and this was worrying him.

Rafe shrugged. "You know as much about Charlie Widmark's records as anybody on the post," he drawled.

"Can't you so much as remember a mention of them roans? Or don't you want to?" The steady look of his pale eyes was deliberately mild.

"You're guessing now." Crouse was sharp. "A poor guess, mister—for all your reputation as a bird dog!"

Baker smiled. "I got more," he offered smoothly. "You and Widmark was pals, I recall. Somebody had to know him awful well to get as close as that killer did. . . . Where was you that night, Lieutenant?" His voice fell to a murmur. "Because I know you was off post, same as Lanark!"

A chill struck through Russ. He was using his poker face now. "You're entirely mistaken," he answered freezingly. "I'm afraid I'll have to propose your replacement, Baker!"

Rafe's sidelong glance was scathing. "Still up to your old tricks, Crouse?" he suggested thinly. "I better warn old Van you'll be gettin' rid of him next!"

Crouse wheeled away, rage pressing his handsome features into an iron mold. But the icy clamp on his heart did not relax. As he entered his quarters he glanced back fleetingly. How much did that infernal scout actually know? Russ had seen too much of Baker's uncanny guesswork to be fooled now. Why had he ever thought Army politics—the heady use of authority—was fun? Money could have afforded him high Government preferment, a life of ease and travel in Europe.

For ten minutes, as he slouched inert on his cot seeing the error of his ways slowly closing about him, Crouse was ready to throw up the whole business. But a streak of willful egotism, long nurtured and seldom curbed, dominated him. Why give up anything he wanted badly enough to scheme for, just because stumbling-blocks like Lanark or Baker stood in his way?

Russ rose up off his cot in a surge of determination, stripping off his gray flannel campaign shirt and yellow-striped blue pants with swift efficiency. In ten minutes he stood clad in civilian garb, being careful not to overdress with his watch-chain, tie and his best boots. Last of all he slipped a service Colt under his belt, tucking it from sight.

Peering out along the parade, he frowned. Rafe Baker still stood on the boardwalk in conversation with a redheaded sergeant of horse. Private sentry duty, beyond a doubt. Crouse whirled back and left by the rear door, making quietly for Colonel VanOsdell's quarters.

"Is the Colonel free?" he asked the colored cook who answered the door.

VanOsdell heard his voice. "That you, Russ? Come in," he invited gruffly. His keen eyes widened at sight of Crouse's dress. "What does this mean, Lieutenant—?"

"Colonel," said Russ hurriedly, slipping inside and standing easily. "I wish to arrange a temporary leave. . . . Scout Baker set me thinking this morning," he hastened on. "I believe I do understand something of Trooper Lanark s habits of mind. With your permission, sir, it's more than possible I may be able to place the man in custody."

"That so? I felt a little sharpness this morning might produce results. . . . What is your plan?"

Crouse displayed awkwardness. "Well, it's—something I'd rather not mention until it proves successful," he evaded. "Could you see your way to letting me work this out my own way, Colonel?"

Believing he read the other's design, the grizzled C.O. merely nodded. "I could and will. . . . If Lanark is returned for court-martial, this may quite probably result in a citation regardless of the outcome," he hinted.

They talked a minute or two longer. But as he walked swiftly away from the interview, Crouse glanced back with a sneer. "Him and his citation," he reflected sarcastically. "It's his own credit he's thinking about!"

Although Russ contemplated leaving Fort McDonald for the last time if matters should work out to his liking, he wasted no sentiment on the dusty parade and sunblasted buildings. Making straight for the administration building, he spotted Dr. Craig's buggy, hitched and standing ready at the far corner. A swift glance showed him various men going about their affairs, none paying attention to him. Freeing the doctor's horse, Russ climbed to the seat and swung the vehicle, driving past the commissary warehouse and into the road leading toward the Agency.

He had time to think before covering the several miles to town. This one-horse rig was decidedly unsuitable to his purpose. Also he preferred to cover his tracks to an extent. Watching warily for any awkward meeting as he drove up the wide street and thankful that Pat Stevens and his cronies did not appear at the moment, Crouse pulled up before the Water Hole saloon, hitched the rig, and stepped briskly inside.

It was not too early to call for a drink. Doing so, Russ waved Cade Grimes forward, sliding the bottle toward him. "How's tricks?" he greeted familiarly.

"No good." Grimes was sullen. "Crispel sacked me, Lieutenant. Says I wasn't mindin' his affairs!" He snorted.

Russ took it in stride. "What of it? Jobs can be found." He was scornfully cheerful. "In fact, I'll help you there. Meanwhile here's a double eagle for a small chore right now."

Tossing the coin over, and lowering his voice, he instructed Grimes to hire a team and buckboard from Lindauer's livery. "Tie it behind Gundel's barn, Grimes, and then drive Doc Craig's buggy back out to the post for me. Will you do that?"

Cade's pig eyes gleamed. He scented shady work, but that was no bar to earning a dollar. After a few more words he finished his drink and sauntered out.

Ten minutes later Russ Crouse guided the hired buckboard onto the Gallup trail, chuckling to himself. "Let Baker unravel that one," he murmured.

Reaching the turn-off to the Bar H, he swung the team that way. He drove more slowly now, his gaze narrowed by speculation. What he was contemplating might take some careful arrangement. But matters turned out far better than he could have expected as, rounding the high ledge at the end of a ridge, he came upon Libby Haskins riding toward him on her favorite bay pony.

Russ pulled up, yanking off his hat and propping a boot

on the dash. "Well, howdy, ma'am." His engaging grin stamped the facetious greeting for what it was.

"Why, Russ!" She was startled by his unheralded appearance out of uniform. "Has something happened—?"

"Only that I'm inviting you for a ride, Lib. I've a good reason this time—news too."

She rode close, obviously trusting him completely and attracted by his presence. "News? What is it? Not a promotion, Lieutenant?" Libby had a coaxing smile of her own. She showed it now.

"No crowding the witness," he ruled. "This is a bargain, lady. Unsaddle that bronc and throw your hull in the wagon—then climb aboard. . . . And don't fret. That pony will find its way home."

Libby plainly wanted to comply, yet she demurred. "If he sees it Father will wonder. He—worries about me," she explained self-consciously.

"With the saddle off?" Crouse scoffed. "Come on—let me help you, Libby. Or back to the post I go, news and all!"

She did not protest as he stripped off the light saddle, heaved it into the buckboard and lifted her up. Springing to the seat, he swung the vehicle about and sent it bowling along the trail, grinning at her.

"Russ," she began soberly after some exchange of small talk, "why *are* you out of uniform today?"

Her seriousness gave him pause. "That's part of the news. . . . It's a pretty sure thing," he announced slowly, choosing his words, "that I'm being transferred to Montana. Oh, I won't leave without telling you about it!" he broke off, noting her expression.

"Russ!" Her tone was low. "You have been transferred already, haven't you? You've—got your orders!" she exclaimed on a note of resignation.

Crouse nodded with pretended unwillingness. "I have," he admitted. He turned to her impulsively. "Libby, why can't you marry me and go along? . . . We've talked it over. You made a thousand weak objections. If we do it right now we can forget it and enjoy life. I'll have a good post in Montana. Fort Snelling—with Army women on post, and many privileges you can't expect here in the desert. In a year or two I'll ask to be transferred East. We'll see big cities—St. Louis—maybe Washington!"

His urgent voice tried hard to sweep her away. And Libby was obviously tempted. Yet she unaccountably found a bar to these light-hearted plans. "We'd—have to get Dad's consent first of all," she ruled firmly. "I simply can't leave him without a word. It's—impossible."

"Oh well." Crouse's enthusiasm suffered a cold check. "We can write him a letter I suppose—maybe visit him someday." He appeared deeply vexed.

"No." The girl was resolute. "This is one thing I must do. . . . Turn the horses, Russ. If you really wish it, we can have it over with in two hours. I—I'll need clothes—"

But he refused. "Take it or leave it, Lib! I can't tell you why; but it's got to be either now or not at all," he brought out flatly.

"Then I must refuse." She sounded choked, and at the same time oddly final. "Russ, what makes you so determined to ignore my reasonable, and perhaps my last serious, request?"

He gazed away briefly, stony-faced. "I didn't want to tell this." His tone was grimly dogged. "It's—that worthless Lanark, girl. He's gone renegade, knowing what's waiting for him if he's captured."

A veil passed over Libby's eyes. Her words were muffled. "What about Flint—?"

"Word reached the post through an Indian," he lied, improvising smoothly. "Lanark has sworn to kill us both if we marry—do you understand, Libby? He hopes to stand in our way, the abandoned fool! . . . But we needn't listen to that," he proceeded with vigor. "Once we're out of New Mexico he'll never find us. It's you I'm really worried about. But don't you see?" He was pleading craftily now. "Involve your father in this business and you're exposing him to the risk of murder. By a crazy madman!"

Libby heard out with widening eyes this rapidly sketched picture of a Flint Lanark she had never known and did not recognize. A keener perception than the officer's would have noted the coldness of her expression.

"Russ." The word dropped into the oily flow of his talk like a stone. Libby straightened her back, turning to confront him squarely. "I'm sorry. I can't believe a word you're saying. I've known Flint Lanark from a boy—and he simply isn't like that at all."

Crouse whirled on her fiercely. "Now you're talking foolish! You simply don't know! Lanark hates my guts—he'd do anything to smash me. Even to killing—which is nothing new for him now!"

"Possibly." She was able to equal his abrupt hostility. "You know best what you've done to make Flint hate you. It *is* like him to retaliate. But not with my help. . . . Take me home," she exclaimed. "Whatever may happen, Mr. Crouse, I insist on time to think it over very carefully!"

Chest swelling arrogantly, he leered at her. "Giving me orders already, are you? I guess not. Start thinking right now, woman—because it's the only chance you'll get!"

She lurched to her feet. "Stop the horses. Or I'll jump!" Her small chin was rigid in a determination that matched her snapping eyes.

For answer Crouse reached out and slammed her roughly back into the seat. "Stay where you are," he bellowed, exhibiting a mask of outrage and fury.

Shrunk small in the corner of the seat, she watched him steadily while he stung the horses to a faster pace. She was frightened but not subdued. "You show yourself plainly, Russ Crouse," she brought out. "I believe you schemed and plotted deliberately to place Flint Lanark where he is—outcast and charged with murder!" Libby realized bitterly, now that her eyes were opened, the extent of her unconscious betrayal of Flint, whose loyalty to her had never been in question. Russ shot her a savage glare.

"Talk away, you vixen!" he snapped. "Believe what you want! If you think you can lead me along and get away with it, here's where you learn different."

The girl rode for a long time without response, her face

remote and closed and her dread growing. Noon came and passed, the buckboard rattling over the stony road. After a time Libby started to talk again, in an effort to probe his true intentions. But now Crouse was grimly sarcastic.

"You'll go my way and like it," he rasped. "Time answers questions—so why should I bother?"

The afternoon was worse. To Libby it seemed endless. Once more she sought to escape by leaping from the wagon, and this time he let her go. They were in the middle of endless, waterless desolation. Russ wheeled the team and followed composedly as she turned back. He dogged her out into the brush with a mocking laugh. Half an hour of this served to defeat even her stout resistance.

"I'll—ride," she gave in at last.

"You will, eh? Climb aboard," was his callous answer, his hard eyes gleaming with malice. He stopped, but did not offer to help her up. Libby sank into the seat, utterly crushed. The silence thereafter was filled with open hatred which the renegade officer shrugged off indifferently.

The sun burned out at long last, and in yellow evening light the girl was aware that they had reached Escondido, a drab baked settlement thirty miles from McDonald. It seemed very unlikely anyone would know they had come this way. Libby must depend solely on her own resources for aid. She looked about her warily.

Russ noted it. His iron grip crushed her arm with deliberate cruelty. "Talk out of turn and I won't answer for what happens," he warned tightly. She could only let that threat sink down through her rising panic.

Crouse pulled up before a run-down boardinghouse. He tethered the horses and elaborately helped Libby down under the eyes of on-lookers, fastening a tight clamp on her elbow. "Do as you're told and keep that lip buttoned," he muttered warningly.

They moved into the cluttered, dirty office. The proprietor, an obese, greasy man who might have been a breed and whose appearance made the girl shiver, nodded stolidly. Crouse didn't seem to notice.

"Overnight guests, friend," he announced in his best

military voice. "Have my rig taken care of, will you—and I'll be needing adjoining rooms for myself and wife."

"Yes, sir." The evil-eyed breed ducked obsequiously, scenting a fat fee.

18

PICKING UP both room-keys, Crouse slanted a look at the expectant proprietor. "Where's the nearest bar?"

"Two doors up." The man jerked a thumb. "While you're about it, neighbor, lead your team through the alley. Barn's in back."

Russ hesitated. But opposing Libby was dry work, and he was not finished yet. A drink might put him in the mood. "Show my wife to her room," he ordered. "I'll be back in five minutes."

The breed nodded. "Come ahead, lady—"

Libby followed, her hands and feet turning cold. She was painfully conscious of Crouse's boots stamping out the door. Numbly she went up a dark and odorous stairway to the barren hallway above.

The breed was unlocking a pine door when she stopped him. "Sir—please." She gave a quick, timid smile. "Would you do me a favor—?"

He looked at her aloofly. She noted his porky jowls, dirty with stubble above the collarless shirt, but hastened on. "It's been a trying day. My—husband is impetuous," she said swiftly. "He'll drink, and then he beats me!"

The man's grunt was unfeeling. He was no stranger to the seamy side of life. "Should've thought of that, lady," was his unhelpful reply.

"But, sir—please!" Libby looked on the verge of crying. "Couldn't you give me a single room—one to myself? It's all I ask."

The breed paused. It was a chance to charge more, and

he had no personal interest in what the loud-voiced guest thought or did. "Well . . . don't blame me if your husband rows yuh," he capitulated. Fishing another key from his pocket, he opened a door in the corner.

Making sure that she got possession of the key, and slipping inside at once, Libby was so elated by momentary success that she paid no heed to the tiny, boxlike room, tightly closed and all but suffocating. Locking herself in, she tried to relax and found she could not. The rattletrap building was far from sound-proof. Hearing masculine voices, a rough laugh, and the stamp of boots she began to dread Crouse's return.

It came soon enough. A man ran heavily upstairs, banged doors, and began to curse. It was Russ. She went cold while he rushed back downstairs bellowing. High words rang up the stairwell, and Crouse thumped back up to bang savagely at her door. "Libby, are you there? Come out!" he bawled. In the face of silence he rattled the door violently, then kicked it. He paid no heed to the breed's yell from below-stairs, his voice rising imperiously.

"Libby!" he thundered. "Will you let me in—?"

She was frightened into a reply. "No—go away!"

Having won this much from her, Russ tried harder. It availed him nothing. He cursed violently and fell into ominous silence. She knew he was scheming, and she began to tremble uncontrollably. But after a time she caught the betraying creak as he sought to tiptoe away.

He was gone for an hour, while she fought in vain for composure. Suddenly his voice shocked her again, when she had no idea he was near. "Libby, how long will this go on?" he snarled. "You can't keep it up! . . . At least come out for your supper!"

"Go away," she managed to say, moving as far as possible from the door. "I couldn't—choke down a thing! Leave me, please—and go. I'll not come out."

Russ reasoned with her. He swore, he pretended to rave. "You'll regret this when I bust that door in," he threatened. All of which failed utterly to move her except in the direction of panic. She refused to answer again, not trusting her unsteady voice, and at length the disgruntled man gave up.

He was back once more at a late hour, probably after a morose evening in the bar. This time, although as far from sleep as ever, Libby did not answer at all, and Crouse's efforts to make her respond called down a flurry of harsh cries from the other roomers, demanding silence. At last Crouse stole away, as furtive as ever.

Exhaustion overcame the girl as she sat in her stiff-backed chair by the shuttered window. Pale daylight was stealing in when a series of thundering knocks jerked her broad awake. She started up wildly. But this time it was not Crouse. "Lady—you stayin' in there all day?" came the breed proprietor's muffled and plaintive query.

Relief flooded through her. "I—don't know. I feel ill," she managed in a trembling voice. "Could you—is there a doctor in town?"

"Hey? Oh . . . There's a horse doctor, lady. Patches gunshot wounds and the like—"

"Get him, please. Bring him here. And hurry!" Libby was clutching at any straw. "I'm afraid he's needed—"

The breed lumbered off, and while she waited she was deathly afraid Russ Crouse would return. But at length there was a moderate knock at the door.

"Who is it—?" Libby made certain it was the M.D. before she opened up. Old Doc Straight was by no means the raw veterinary she expected. "What's your trouble, sister?" His pleasant eyes crinkled shrewdly. They opened wider when Libby carefully relocked the door, but he waited for an explanation.

"Doctor, I'm in serious trouble," she burst out at once. "Have you an office?"

His watching nod was sober.

"Take me there at once," she pleaded urgently. "I must get away from here! I'm being abducted."

Doc, his shrewd eyes narrowed to slits by now, insisted that she seat herself. "This is a professional call. You're nervous and upset, I see that." He examined her briefly, then clucked his tongue. "Worse than I thought. . . .

Have to conduct you to my office for diagnosis. Then I'll
—uh—prescribe."

"Please do that, will you, Doctor?" She rose as he did.
"And—don't let anyone interfere!"

His grunt was reassurance. They passed down the rough
stairs, Libby stumbling in her excitement, and moved out
through the office to the street. Still Russ Crouse did not
appear. Russ was in fact caught so flat-footed that when
he ran into them several doors below he allowed old Doc
to bluff him out of their path.

Seeing the weathered frame house with Straight's shin-
gle at the side door, Libby almost ran toward its protection. Doc bundled her in breezily, turned her to the left
into his cluttered office and sank into a bursting leather-
bound chair with a sigh. "Now, young lady," he declared.
"You're absolutely safe here. Let's have that story—"

Sinking into the chair opposite, she rushed into her nar-
rative so nervously that Doc had to break in repeatedly
with questions. He had heard rumors of the trouble at
McDonald, and was shrewd enough to put two and two
together. By further effort he managed to extract a fairly
comprehensive tale.

"This Crouse we met." He steepled his chubby fingers,
peering at her over his glasses. "You say he's an Army
officer?"

She repeated Russ's story of his transfer. "Does that
account for his being out of uniform, Doctor? I see you
noticed."

"I doubt it, girl." His lips pursed. "There's something
funny here. . . . And that Lanark you mentioned. He's
in—hiding—too?"

She looked at him in amazement. "Doctor! You don't
think Mr. Crouse could have been using me for . . .
bait?" She was deeply shocked.

Doc's chuckle was amused. "An old sawbones like me
ain't much surprised by anything. I've met old Joe Haskins, too—and if you're like him, girl, it won't you!"

Before more could be said there came an insistent tugging at the bell-wire. Doc Straight conscientiously closed
the office door when he went to answer. She heard only

muffled masculine voices, which set her heart thumping
unaccountably. Doc was deliberately serene when he came
back after a considerable delay. But his eyes flashed with
anger.

"It was him——?" she breathed.

He blinked at her mildly. "Your lieutenant, you mean?
Yes. He insisted on seeing you. I refused. Doctor's privilege, you know."

"What will he do?" she whispered.

At that moment Russ was planning with savage vigor
just what his next move would be. "I'll put a spoke in that
damned pill-roller's wheel," he muttered bitterly. He
halted the first reputable looking citizen met on the street,
asking directions for finding the town marshal. Later, as
he approached a shack near the edge of town, he saw a
sleepy-eyed, gangling individual languidly sweeping the
doorstep.

"Marshal Coskey? . . . Lieutenant Crouse, from Mc-
Donald," he introduced himself at the other's nod. "Sorry
to bother you with Army affairs, but this seems to be a
case where civil law is involved."

Coskey waited. He recognized the military bearing,
the clipped speech, and was ready enough to accept the
other at face value.

"I'm on rather an awkward private mission, in fact. I'd
just as soon it didn't get past you." Russ dropped his
voice confidentially. "I arrived in town with a woman in
custody, Marshal. . . . Wife of a fellow officer—Lieutenant Griffin. She— Well, the truth is, Coskey, she tried to
run off with a scoundrel. It's a long story, of course; the
upshot is that I got her away from him and am taking her
back to her husband."

Improvising smoothly, Crouse spun out his lie with
suave plausibility. He added a few details reflecting no
credit on Libby, and smugly congratulated himself when
the lawman's jaw dropped open, then shut with a click. It
was going over.

"The woman would like to strangle me if she could,"
he continued. "You can picture her state of mind, Coskey
—still in love with that unprincipled rat! She must have

been planning all the while she was crying and explaining herself to me; and the minute we reached town she acted."

From this point he was able to relate almost exactly what had occurred overnight. It fitted admirably into his tale, even to the girl's worming her way into the doctor's confidence, probably with some far-fetched story of her own.

From his indignant look, Coskey accepted the unlovely picture even more completely than Russ had dared hope. "Reckon yuh got a problem on your hands," he growled. "What do yuh want me to do, Lieutenant?"

"I was hoping you could make Doc Straight see the light and turn my troublesome charge over to me," replied Crouse. "Thank heaven I'll soon land her where she belongs, and be rid of her," he added the pious comment.

It persuaded Coskey. Standing the broom inside the door, he hitched up his gunbelt purposefully. "We'll see, we'll see. Come along with me, Lieutenant."

They marched upstreet to the doctor's office. The marshal banged on the door officiously. It was a minute or two before Doc appeared, opening the door partially. He scowled at sight of them. "What yuh after, Coskey?"

"I want in, Doc." The marshal gave the door a vigorous shove. "Yuh know very well what I want. Open up!"

Doc sputtered angrily, retreating a foot or two. "This is forcible entry, Coskey; and what's more it's damned bad manners," he protested strongly. "Yuh got a search warrant? This is private property, I'll remind yuh—"

Coskey laughed at him harshly. "Nonsense. This is a business office, Doc—and we got business with yuh."

Straight did not miss the plural, his eye flicking venomously over Crouse. Keenly aware of what was afoot, he stalled. "*You* can come in," he conceded grudgingly.

Gaining his point, Coskey thrust forward, crowding the medico toward the office door. "Go on—go on," he urged gruffly. "We'll have this out whether yuh like it or not!"

Libby was standing with her back against an untidily jammed bookcase when they entered, her hands tightly clasped, her eyes frightened. She refused to turn toward Russ, but she had a grip on herself. "That's the man who's trying to abduct me, Doctor," she said clearly.

Coskey's chuckle grated flatly. "Still tryin' to work your game, are yuh?" he retorted admiringly, examining the girl with critical coldness.

"Just what are *you* drivin' at?" snapped Doc huffily.

"Careful, Doc," the lawman warned. "That woman's an Army wife, runnin' off from her husband. The Lieutenant here caught up with her, and he's takin' her home. I don't know what story she told yuh—but right now you're standin' in the way of Army brass."

Libby sucked in her breath sharply. "What an outrageous story!" she exclaimed hotly. "I warned you, Doctor, this man will say anything to gain his ends." She was able to look at Crouse now, her eyes blazing with contempt.

"Come, come, Mrs. Griffin," Coskey said impatiently. "Yuh must know these lies will hold up for only so long—"

"*Mrs. Griffin?* My name is Libby Haskins, from the Bar H outside of Fort McDonald. I tell you I am not married and have no wish to be!"

The stolid indifference with which Marshal Coskey and Russ Crouse heard her out had its effect. Even Doc was startled into momentary uncertainty. "You *are* Joe Haskins' daughter, girl?" he begged urgently.

Libby felt herself go cold. She had cause to know Crouse's diabolical plausibility only too well. There was still the possibility that he might succeed in persuading these men, to her cost. One single expedient remained— to take a leaf out of his own book and press home the attack with all the resolution she could muster.

"While you're doubting me, you might better question exactly who the Lieutenant is!" she exclaimed scathingly.

The marshal eyed her bleakly. "Know that. His name's Crouse—from McDonald," he grunted.

"Then I can tell you something you don't know about him." She leveled a finger dramatically at Russ. "He's deeply involved in the murder of Adjutant Widmark—and right now, Marshal, you're assisting in his escape!"

Coskey looked blank in the sudden silence. Yet he was not overly impressed. "How do yuh figure that?" he rasped.

"Are you perfectly accustomed to seeing Army officers out of uniform?" she shot back. "Are you so sure his 'fellow officer's' sad story would have any effect on his commanding officer? . . . It would be far more like him to run off with some officer's wife himself. Look at that handsome profile, Marshal!"

An electric tension filled the room. She was doing far better than she had dared hope, despite Crouse's look of bored tolerance. Still Coskey was by no means wholly sold.

"Why is he draggin' you around—since you're tellin' so much?" he demanded.

"Because I know too much about him! I'm his 'protection'—till he can get out of the country and abandon me!"

There was a deadly logic in all this which finally jarred Crouse out of his pained superiority. His laugh was a caustic bark—and it was forced. "Have you had enough yet, Coskey?" he threw at the marshal. "I warned you she was using woman's wiles. Too damned clever for her own good!" He appeared sternly intent on sweeping all nonsense aside. "I'll get up my rig," he broke off practically, "and get started for McDonald with this—this parcel of grief!" He glanced at Libby in hatred.

"No—hold on." Coskey was suddenly and unexpectedly stubborn. "I ain't swallowin' this crazy yarn of hers for a minute, Lieutenant. But to me either story's as crazy as the other," he reminded candidly. "What's your sweat? If you're tellin' the truth, the loss of a day or two can't do no great harm."

Crouse stared in disbelief, his scalp crawling. "Just what does that mean?" he demanded imperiously.

"It means we'll hold yuh both here for a spell while I check with the Army," Coskey told him with steady finality.

Russ felt the same cold chill he had experienced in the face of Rafe Baker's shrewd questioning. Any remote connection with Widmark's fate, even by implication, was the last thing he could afford. Slowly but surely he felt the web of circumstance closing tighter and tighter.

"But that's preposterous—!" Protesting gruffly, he moved closer to Coskey, a hand extended.

"Could be, Lieutenant." The marshal's face was stony. "One way or another, we'll soon know."

Unwarningly, Crouse went into action. A vicious sweep of his boot knocked Coskey's feet out from under him and sent him crashing down. There was no time to reach Libby. Russ savagely stiff-armed Doc backward against a shelf of jingling glass and leaped to the door. A single wrench of the handle and he was gone.

19

"THAT ROTTEN Crouse is behind this!" exclaimed Flint Lanark when Stevens hurriedly called out from the door the news of Libby's disappearance. "Holy smoke! Here I was ready to wait till morning—!"

He barged into the Bar H house, careless now of who saw him, firing questions at the dismayed rancher to satisfy himself that Libby was nowhere to be found. "What did she say?" he barked, turning back from her empty room after a brisk search. "Did she talk about Crouse at all?"

The answer was no. "Ain't heard his name for two or three days, and I was hopin' she'd forgot him." Old Joe's eyes were haggard and pleading. "She rode in to town yesterday afternoon and didn't get back. I figured she got to visitin'—she does that. . . . Blast it all! Why didn't I insist on goin' with her?"

No one questioned the strong probability that Russ Crouse was behind it all. "That ape overreached himself this time," Flint raged. "We'll ride to the fort right now, Stevens—get hold of the Old Man and force a show-down!"

His readiness to ignore his own dilemma was full proof of his great concern. Pat shook his head decidedly. "No —that's all Crouse needs right now to make him happy. You'll stay here, Lanark," he ruled. "And I'll leave Ez here with you. Sam and I will go to McDonald and see what we can learn."

Ezra saved time by proceeding to get up fresh horses for the pair. Flint wanted to argue; yet he had faith in Pat's judgment. "Just hurry it up, Stevens!" he begged. "And don't let old Van talk you out of this—"

Pat and Sloan got away a few minutes later. They thrust forward steadily, arriving at the fort in early morning darkness. A sentry challenged them sharply at the edge of the parade-ground. They identified themselves but had to wait.

"Corp'ral of the guard! Post number eight!"

A robust non-com finally appeared, flanking the guard. "All right, you two. What is it—?"

"Important information for the Colonel, Corporal," Pat responded. "It can't wait—unless you say so!"

The inference was plain. The disgruntled corporal stepped back. "Pass, friend," he growled.

Leaving the horses, they skirted officer's row and made for Colonel VanOsdell's isolated cottage. A guard stepped out of the darkness under the porch.

"Halt! Who goes there?"

"We've got to see the Colonel at once, soldier," Pat declared curtly. "Call him out, will you?"

This time they found a hardier spirit to deal with. "Not a chance! Turn around and march, mister. Orders are the Colonel's not to be disturbed except for—" The guard broke off, peering hard at Sam. "*Is* that Trooper Lanark you've got with yuh?"

"Not unless he's got awful short and fat," Sam an-

swered for himself dryly. "But this is important! Get Van-
Osdell out here fast, son."

Perhaps his tone was the wrong one. The guard's rigidly presented carbine did not waver. "No admittance,"
he snapped. "Sheer off—or get the proper authority!"

Stevens gave over, pulling Sam away. "Take it easy.
He's got his orders," he muttered. "Now, if only we knew
where to locate Rafe Baker in a hurry—"

"Shucks. I can figure that one. Wait here, Stevens."

He faded into the darkness before Pat could call him
back. Ten minutes passed. The Lazy Mare owner was
expecting an uproar at any moment, when a soft voice
spoke at his shoulder. "What is it now, Stevens?"

Pat made out the Army scout's shadowy form. "We've
got to reach VanOsdell right now, Baker. You should
know how—"

"Locate Lanark, did yuh?"

Pat did not even hesitate. "Yes—but this doesn't concern him."

His complete frankness did it. The scout cupped a
hand beside his mouth. "Corp'ral of the guard!" he sang
out.

A bare moment served this time to bring the irate non-
com hurrying. "What the devil now?" he began, all the
more forceful for having to suppress his voice near the
Colonel's cottage. "Oh . . . That you, Bake? Hang it
all—!"

Baker thumbed toward the guard. "Tell that monkey
I'm seein' the Colonel," he directed briefly, with the hard
authority of a commissioned officer. The properly impressed corporal barked a command. The guard withdrew. "Come on, Stevens," Baker said.

Sam waited while the pair moved up on the cottage
porch and knocked. Then they were let in.

Colonel VanOsdell lost nothing of his native dignity,
tucking his nightshirt into his pants as he met them in the
soft gleam of a hastily lit coal oil lamp. Pat spoke up at
once. "Sorry to disturb you, Colonel. I'm forced to inquire at once into the whereabouts of Lieutenant Crouse,"
he began firmly.

VanOsdell looked at him sharply, then at Baker. "Lieutenant Crouse? He's on leave," he said shortly.

Pat nodded. "We gathered that much. I was hoping you could say where."

Perfectly aware they had not awakened him at such an hour without a serious reason, the C.O. hesitated. "I suppose these questions have a purpose, gentlemen—"

Pat's smile had no vestige of humor in it. "Joe Haskins' daughter has disappeared, sir. The lieutenant is known to have paid his—attentions to her."

VanOsdell sobered. A far from stupid man, he chose to ignore the ominous significance of these facts. "That's —true. Perhaps they eloped," he evaded gruffly. "Have you thought of that, Stevens?"

Pat's nod was curt. "I thought of it. And turned it down."

Still the grizzled officer was not inclined to meddle. "If you're convinced they're together, what do you think has happened?" he countered expressionlessly.

"The question is, what has happened to that girl, Colonel. Haskins certainly has the right to know. And I want to also."

VanOsdell avoided Pat's level gaze, scratching his beard dubiously. "I don't suppose it's anything serious—"

Watching him dourly, Baker spoke up. "Stevens thinks Crouse's reason for askin' leave will answer that—if you don't get it, Colonel."

VanOsdell entertained considerable respect for the judgment of his scout, and he answered carefully. "There are military reasons why I don't consider myself obliged to answer that," he said gruffly.

Baker glanced significantly at Pat. "Thought so. What more do yuh want, Stevens?" was his terse comment.

"All right, Colonel. Then I'll tell you," Pat spoke up forcefully. "We know search patrols are out looking for Trooper Lanark. I think Crouse offered to locate your man and pick him up—and I think he's using that girl as bait!" His tone said what he thought of any such procedure not authorized by known military precedent.

"Crouse pulled out yesterday in Doc Craig's buggy," supplied Baker mildly. "He was out of uniform. . . . Doc was pretty mad."

The Colonel threw out his hands. "Well—well!" he exclaimed irritably. "Maybe it was like that. There's still no proof that Lieutenant Crouse is using any such methods as you suggest!" he protested mildly.

Pat met his look squarely. "I told you that Libby Haskins has disappeared, sir. If you draw no meaning from that, we'll be forced to take action on our own responsibility. Your knowledge of the lieutenant's object must inform you of whether elopement was on his mind—or something else."

VanOsdell nodded slowly. "Russ did declare to me that he believed he could bring Trooper Lanark in," he owned reluctantly. "It was my duty to accept such an offer— and I regret now that I failed to ask him how. I . . . appreciate your concern for Miss Haskins. Are you asking for help, Stevens?"

Pat shrugged. "Only your full support when the facts are laid in front of you," he answered bluntly. "We know now where we stand. Thank you, Colonel."

He was ready to leave. "Good luck in your search— and keep me posted, will you?" VanOsdell urged gruffly as the two men turned away.

Whatever their thoughts, neither Pat nor Baker said anything as they let themselves out. Sam met them in the compound. "Any luck?" he growled.

"At least we know what we're up against." Pat was unusually terse. "Russ Crouse is sly and crooked—it's my opinion he's the killer to boot. In the clutch, we'll pin that on him too!"

Listening carefully, the lean, dry Army scout declined to argue. "Crouse may be gone awhile," he ventured. "His orderly Shreeve told me Russ left some personal belongings with him—"

Pat considered this briefly. "That's an idea. Stick around, will you, Sam? Contact that sergeant and try for a look at Crouse's things. They may tell us plenty."

Sam was dismayed. "Hold on, now," he protested. "Can't Rafe do that for yuh?"

Baker shook his head. "Goin' with Stevens," was all he said.

The gray light of dawn was strengthening in the east when Pat and the scout rode away from the fort. Though they traveled steadily, it was full daylight long before they reached the barren hills hemming in the Bar H.

At a curve where the trail rounded a rocky dyke, Flint Lanark rode boldly out to join them. "Didn't learn much, did you," he snorted. "At least you used good judgment, bringing Baker along."

Rafe showed no surprise whatever at Lanark's appearance. "All right. What are you braggin' about, boy?" he countered shrewdly.

"At dawn Ez found what he says are buckboard tracks," supplied Flint hardily. "Him and old Joe are trailin' after now. I waited for you. Shall we shove along?" Impatience roughened his tone.

Pat waved a hand. "Lead off, Lanark."

They swung out across the brushy desert and presently turned into the Escondido trail. During the dark hours Flint had found time to supply himself with bacon sandwiches and a canteen from Libby's kitchen. The trio forced down a bite as they rode.

Half an hour later Baker mounted a small rise and pointed. "Stray bronc," he announced.

They swept out to corner it. Lanark gulped. "It's Libby's," he declared. "See them sweat marks? Saddle's been stripped off—"

They knew they were on the right track. Without more words they turned at once to pursue the sandy wagon trail over the long barren swells. Toward midmorning they spotted tiny figures far ahead, and in twenty minutes they overtook Haskins and Ezra.

"Took long enough," grumbled Ez, tired of restraining the rancher's impatience. "Where's Sam?"

Pat explained. Haskins turned pain-dulled eyes to note

Baker's presence. He nodded civilly, but nothing was said about their common mission. No sign of the buckboard had been seen, and they pressed forward in haste to reach Escondido.

The sun-baked little settlement appeared far off across the dun level. If they did not increase their pace it was because their midday shadows lay directly underneath them now, and the heat was oppressive.

Escondido lay on the last dry strip beside the rising humps of a gashed and crumbling badlands stretching off to the north. From a quarter-mile away they could look down its wide, almost deserted street. As they plodded steadily on, they could not help asking themselves what manner of problem this town would present. Had the fleeing Crouse hauled up here—or driven straight on through? They might be forced to the expedient of many time-consuming inquiries and yet learn little or nothing.

As it happened, however, matters worked out more expeditiously than they could have hoped. They were just approaching the near end of the street, with Stevens mapping a tentative plan of campaign in his mind, when Ez lifted his hand and pointed.

"Hey! Look at that—"

As they watched, a man suddenly leaped off the porch of an isolated frame house some distance up the street and raced at top speed across toward the horse rack opposite. It was the work of a second to free a tethered saddle horse. Swarming astride as he whirled the animal, the man kicked it into a mad run and tore on up the street toward the open desert in a cloud of shimmering dust.

Startled by this unexpected exhibition they rammed their horses forward. They were in time to catch the harsh yell of a man who sprang out of a supply store, waving an irate fist. "Stop that horse thief!" he bawled.

A dozen men were in the street and more were hurrying forward by the time Pat's party cantered hastily up to join them.

"We seen that," Ez called loudly. "The buzzard came jumpin' out of that house yonder! He run across, grabbed the bronc and took off—" His single eye raked the angry faces searchingly. "Who was it? Do any of yuh know?"

They looked at him blankly, more than one shaking his head. Pat had just noticed Doc Straight's sign when a lanky individual hurried out of the door. He wore a marshal's badge on his sagging vest, and he looked flustered and furious, having lost his hat.

"I know him," he shouted. "That tricky hombre rode into town last night in a buckboard! Claimed to be an officer from McDonald—but that's probably a lie."

It was all the five needed to assure them the fugitive was indeed Crouse. Pat whirled, crowding his bronc close to Lanark's. "We'll take his trail. Stay here, boy—see if you can locate Libby. I don't want to hear any arguments, now!"

Flint, however, was already gauging with new eyes what the town had to offer. "So get on with it, Stevens! What are yuh waitin' for?" he barked.

During this exchange a man came forward with a led horse. "Gimme that bronc!" Marshal Coskey grabbed at the reins and swung up. He rammed the pony into action and was in the lead as Pat and his three companions fell in to race up the street in the direction the fugitive had gone.

Giving scant attention to their departure, Lanark swung to the ground. He hitched up his belt and glanced about. "Anybody see a girl with that skunk in the buckboard?" he demanded.

It happened that none had. But while these range men were feverishly making ready to join the pursuit, an elderly merchant was busy remembering. "Say! Lebeau was grumblin' about some woman at his place last night—the boardin' house yonder. Then I seen Doc Straight hustle down there this mornin'. Didn't notice after that. . . . Why not tackle Doc?" he proposed quickly.

Flint eyed the doctor's house, nodding sternly. "That'll do for a start."

He strode across, stepping agilely aside as a posse on hastily procured mounts swept up the street in the wake of Coskey and the others. The doctor's door stood open. Stepping in, Lanark came up against the closed office door, which stopped him only momentarily. Lifting a fist, he banged on it heavily.

"Who's that, now?" Straight's voice was sharp.

The door appeared to be fastened, but the thrust of a brawny knee snapped the catch and sent it shuddering open. Startled, Libby met Lanark's burning gaze for a bare second, then rushed swiftly into his arms.

"Oh, Flint!" she cried fervently. "I wondered if you would ever come!"

It told him all he wished to know about her feelings. He gathered her close. "Are you all right, Libby?" He was hoarse with anxiety.

"Yes," she assured quickly, her voice threatening to break now that the ordeal was over. "Thanks to the doctor, I have only a nightmare ride to remember—"

"Then it *was* Crouse?" His tone shook with anger.

She could only nod. "Is he—?"

"Don't worry, girl." Lanark had taken charge for good, his manner sternly protective. "Crouse stole a bronc and ran. But Pat Stevens is hot after him—and Rafe Baker—and those Bar ES hellions! . . . He won't get far!"

There was deep significance packed in the cryptic comment, but neither Doc nor Libby asked for an explanation.

20

It was immediately obvious that Russ Crouse was headed directly for the badlands since the deeply gouged tracks of the stolen pony marked his course unmistakably. Stevens could not fathom why the renegade officer, who apparently had been following the trail west across open desert, had abruptly swerved off and headed straight for the wildly broken hills.

Marshal Coskey overshot the turn, and Baker called him back while Ez and Pat swung out to follow the hot trail. The way led straight through the ragged brush. "What's he up to now?" the one-eyed man rasped alertly, fully aware of the quarry's wily nature.

"Either he figures to break his sign in a hurry, or he saw something back there!" Pat hauled his running horse to a buck-jumping halt, waiting for Baker and Coskey to catch up. "Spread out and watch those breaks—in case Crouse doubles back to throw us off," he called, waving toward the rocky gaps and eroded crevices gashing the base of the sullen hills.

They separated, spreading out and scrutinizing the incredibly rough mass of the badlands. It seemed impossible that a horse could get far in that scarred and tortured maze. It had swallowed up Crouse completely; yet even now he might be hidden somewhere along its ragged fringe, only waiting for them to pass on before slipping out and racing to safety.

Less than ten minutes later, at the far end of the line, Pat looked up and spotted a small cavalcade advancing along the edge of the hills. It was an Army detachment, in charge of an erect, downy-cheeked but businesslike second lieutenant.

The troopers thundered forward in a haze of golden

dust. Stevens lifted a hand in careless salute. "Expect you're scouting for Lanark, Lieutenant—"

"That's right." The sun-reddened shavetail nodded, adding carefully, "Just what is your excuse, mister?"

Pat explained about the stolen bronc, at the same time omitting to mention Crouse's identity. "We trailed the thief to these hills twenty minutes ago—and he may be your man." He told where his friends were scattered out. "If you'll throw your patrol around the broken country yonder, we'll soon know."

The under-officer snapped a curt question or two and swiftly concluded he dared not overlook this opportunity. Rapping out orders, he soon cast a wide and steadily closing net of grizzled, hard-eyed campaigners about the badlands.

Watching briefly, Pat understood why Russ Crouse had abruptly gone into hiding in the hills. It could only have been in a panic of consternation that, after all his crafty scheming, the renegade lieutenant found himself forced to flee the very trap he had set for his enemy. His luck was running thin at last, and Pat found it ironical that the service which he sought so coolly to betray should be instrumental in bringing Crouse to book.

When the outer hills were covered he wheeled back and made straight for the first rocky gap, then drove into the broken, weirdly eroded maze of stone. There was no conceivable order or design to this Chinese puzzle of rocks. Stripes and bands of yellow, red and brown, in endless variation, deceived the eye. Crumbling shale rattled under the horse's hoofs and dust puffed up, sharp and choking.

Throwing his gun up as a sliding and crashing sounded somewhere nearby, Pat attempted to read its direction. Lead tore at his hat as the flat roar of a gun sounded almost behind him. He glimpsed Crouse across a series of low humps; the fugitive fired again fruitlessly and, crouching low as he whirled his bronc, fled deeper into the maze.

If Russ flashed from sight in a trice, the sound of his going lingered on the dust-choked air. Far from being betrayed into breakneck pursuit, Pat listened keenly and then started slowly after him. There were so many paths and crannies leading in every direction that he scarcely knew which to follow.

Five minutes later a carbine broke the silence beyond tall towers of sculptured rock. Soon after came the sound of a horse in mad flight. Pat knew what it spelled. Crouse's own troopers had turned him back.

Tensing in readiness, he realized in short order that the quarry was passing at some distance to one side. Stevens wheeled back, knowing the other was making at all speed for the open desert. There was a bare chance of intercepting him, and Pat flashed back down the twisting corridors, managing to keep within sound of Crouse's headlong progress. Then suddenly the thundering, jingling pound of hoofs faded out.

Bursting into the open two minutes later, Pat swept his eyes over the flats. A distant yell sounded. Ezra was waving and pointing toward an indistinguishable hump bobbing along the edge of a shallow wash. Crouse was trying to conceal his flight by crouching low over his pommel. Pat grunted his satisfaction, waving Ez that way and tearing after. At last they had flushed the quarry out of the rough. Russ was giving that up and heading back toward Escondido. What could his object be?

Pat was halfway to town, with Crouse still far in the lead, when a signal gunshot broke from the badlands. Baker had met a trooper and was calling the patrol in. Riders were streaming after Stevens. He knew the scout would order the troopers thrown around the settlement, closing Crouse inside an ever-tightening web.

Crouse had faded from sight amidst the buildings when Pat reached the edge of Escondido. But moments later he overtook the stolen bronc, abandoned in an empty lot, its reins dragging. Crouse had plunged into the snarl of sheds, livery barns and ramshackle warehouses on foot.

Fences blocked Pat's plunging course, and he turned into the street. It was imperative to warn the townspeople. "Lanark—and you others," he called, riding swiftly down on a knot of men before the supply store. "Look alive! We drove our man back—he's here in town now!

He may hide or keep on the move! So—watch yourselves!"

Hearing this, they swiftly scattered out. Flint stared up at Pat fixedly, read his gesture, and dived into an alley. Thirsty for blood, the hard-bitten townsmen speedily demonstrated their fierce enthusiasm for the hunt. Almost at once an uproar of harsh voices broke out behind the saloon. Guns pounded. Then a man burst into the street, gazing about wildly.

"He got away—!"

Between buildings Pat spied the cavalry guard circling town. Wherever he went, Crouse could not slip away. Then upstreet he saw two purposeful figures riding in. One was Sam Sloan. The other— He peered again, startled, recognizing Colonel VanOsdell.

Ez appeared farther down the street, directing men in the frenzied search. Baker was with him, and Marshal Coskey was intent, his Colt in his hand. Pat weighed this setup, then jogged out to meet the Colonel.

"Be careful of yourself, Colonel," he advised bluntly. "They're busy tracking down a horse thief here—and maybe a killer. I might as well warn you he's an Army man—"

"I know, Stevens. Say Lieutenant Crouse, and be done with it!" VanOsdell's trim beard jutted. There was no sign of irresolution in his stern manner. "Cover those alleys, Breen!" he barked as a cavalryman appeared in the street, waving him back.

Pat saw with amazement that the Colonel was taking charge of the stern hunt. "Better warn them all that Crouse is out of uniform, Colonel—and heavily armed."

VanOsdell jerked a nod. "Find that girl, did you?" he changed the subject briefly.

Pat thought Libby was still at the doctor's. "She can stand a guard till this is over with. I'll check now." Hurrying that way, he wondered what would happen should the troopers bump into Lanark, caught unawares in this trap tightening about Russ Crouse.

Pat sprang from the saddle in front of Doc Straight's and glanced back. Colonel VanOsdell had moved to the store steps, where the young lieutenant in charge of the patrol was saluting him. The C.O.'s barked commands came drifting Pat's way.

Pat's hand was stretched out for Doc's door handle when he froze. A tall, rugged-framed figure leaped from the store entrance directly behind VanOsdell. Before he could turn, Russ Crouse jammed a long-barreled pistol into his superior's ribs, a muscular arm pinning the Colonel from behind.

"Call off the wolves, old man, before I blast you down," bawled the renegade.

Rafe Baker appeared almost at once, a trooper or two behind him. Seeing the situation they halted in their tracks at a safe distance. Ez and Sam showed their faces directly across from the store, and armed men began to appear along the street. For this tense minute silence and inactivity held them all.

Although he was boiling in rage at this wholly unexpected predicament, VanOsdell did not turn a hair, nor did he hesitate for longer than a matter of seconds. "Take this man in custody at once," he roared.

The lean, imperturbable Baker held up both hands, promptly countermanding this headlong order before anyone could make an impulsive move. "There's a gun in your back, Colonel, and a fool behind it," the scout said mildly.

"No matter!" The doughty Colonel's wrath was mounting swiftly. "Walk up here and take him in charge! I order you to ignore my safety, do you hear? What are you waiting for?"

"You're under arrest, you!" Marshal Coskey shouted at Crouse without moving a foot to make good his threat. "You won't ever get out of this town! Drop that gun and give yourself up!"

As he hugged his captive close Crouse's blazing face showed only an inhuman resolve. "Order them to leave two horses here—then retire," he grated into VanOsdell's ear, loudly enough for the others to catch. "You're seeing me out of this, Van. Or *you* never will see the end of it!"

VanOsdell struggled ineffectually, snorting in fury. If

Russ thought the other men were spellbound by his peril it was pure miscalculation on his part. Prudence alone held those in his sight from moving from their positions. But minutes ago all except Crouse himself had seen Flint Lanark appear at the corner of the store. Only the greater drama being played out here had prevented an outcry.

Flint crept up the store steps, and while Crouse talked he edged along the porch with soundless caution, his back to the wall. Second by second he drew closer to the renegade. Pat was by now as close as any of the others, twenty yards away across the dust-churned street.

"Dicker with your man, Colonel," he called out, to distract Crouse's needle-sharp attention for another vital moment or two. "If he'll give himself up, promise a fair trial—"

Crouse pretended to ignore this, jabbing the furious C.O. with his gun muzzle. "Pass out those orders, mister," he gritted tightly. "It's you or me!"

The words were barely out when Lanark closed in and swooped down on his prey. One iron fist struck Russ on the side of his neck, the other hand simultaneously knocking the dragoon Colt away from VanOsdell's back. The gun exploded and the slug ploughed into the boards of the porch. Crouse crashed down sidewise, tripping over an artfully placed boot.

He writhed over on his back, snarling. The gun crashed again. Dodging aside, Lanark plunged down at him. "Flint! *Be careful,*" came Libby's horrified cry through the heavy silence.

Lanark immediately grabbed Crouse's gun in both hands, wrenching it away and flinging it aside. Surging up, Crouse sprang straight at Flint's throat. But with VanOsdell no longer in peril, men came charging in from every side. Ruthless hands tore the renegade back, brutally subduing him and rendering him helpless at last.

Libby ran up the steps to Lanark. "Flint, Flint." Her voice choked with relief. "You're so reckless—!"

"Come out of his arms, daughter—for now anyhow!" Joe Haskins was scandalized by this public display. The girl looked at him unmoving, and it was Lanark who stiffly freed himself, turning to face the Colonel with a wooden salute.

"Trooper Lanark, sir. Reporting for—discipline," he said gruffly.

VanOsdell had weathered the past few minutes with notable aplomb. He eyed Lanark shrewdly. "At ease, soldier." He was equally gruff, his next words coming with the effect of a bombshell. "We'll say you were on detached duty—"

There was an instant before the impact of this drove home. Libby gasped. "You mean—Flint is no longer under arrest, Colonel?"

"That's right." The stern C.O. nodded dryly. "You can strip Crouse of his Army credentials and hold him in close custody, Sergeant," he ordered before turning back. "I've been learning fast, ma'am—if I seemed to move slow," he confided to the thunderstruck girl.

"Then you know that Crouse was behind this whole affair, I take it, Colonel?" Pat asked carefully.

"Yes. By putting two and two together," VanOsdell proceeded strictly, "I gathered from Sheriff Lybolt's story that Crouse—the only Army hand in his posse—must have deliberately hoodwinked him by turning those roan strays loose. That seems to have been aimed at landing Trooper Lanark deeper in serious charges, and it nearly worked—"

"Don't quite follow that," allowed Ez critically.

"It stems from the alleged misappropriation of Army stock," the Colonel explained. "Your partner Sloan ironed that out. He came straight to me about the 'personal effects' that Crouse left with his orderly. I had long asked myself what could possibly have happened to Adjutant Widmark's post records. If it's any news, Ezra, they were included in Crouse's luggage—along with the signed order for Lanark to dispose of those roans. I can say now that every move the trooper made was strictly according to orders."

"That's a lie," snarled Crouse arrogantly, bitterly careless now of all authority. "Somebody double-crossed me! That stuff was planted in my bags!"

His orderly, fortunately with the patrol, vigorously jostled him to silence. "What about that, Sergeant?" Van-Osdell demanded pointedly.

Shreeve shrugged. "All I'll say, sir, is that the Lieutenant tried bribin' me to finish off Adjutant Widmark's driver in his hospital bed before he came to and talked—"

"But poor Fenner never did wake up." VanOsdell nodded curtly. "It seems probable that, in this case, his testimony won't be required. . . . That'll do. Proceed to McDonald, Mr. Carson," he told the second lieutenant in charge, "and lodge the prisoner in the guardhouse to await court-martial. This time, I think, there will be little or no delay!"

"Oh, Flint!" Libby was not at all bashful in displaying her full confidence in the embarrassed cavalryman. "You are cleared of every charge, since it's known now that you had no reason to murder Adjutant Widmark! I knew you would be!"

"Every charge, that is," drawled Sam, "except that of triflin' with a girl's affections. . . . Yuh can duck even that one, Lanark," he proceeded ingenuously, "by takin' out a hitchin' license on your first leave—"

"I'll do it, Sloan," Flint declared earnestly, appearing not to notice Libby's quick blush. "My Army hitch ends in the fall. After that I'll get down to serious business, stockin' the Oasis ranch with cows. Libby can help me there, good as a man."

"You'll need horses too. We better leave yuh two or three for a weddin' present," said Ez, not without design, as he turned to glance inquiringly at the Colonel. "I expect we'll be allowed to drive them roans home to Powder Valley where they belong now, eh?" he inquired lightly.

VanOsdell took the hint with a brief smile. "That's right. In a pinch, boys, the service can spare Corporal Lanark long enough to help with the drive," he announced. "Unless, of course, he finds something more important to occupy him for ten days—"

Flint and Libby looked startled. A change in rating, with the consequent raise in pay, would mean much to them. "I—thank you, Colonel, sir!" Largely unused to frank sentiment, the cavalryman was covered with brief confusion.

"It's time I got back to the Lazy Mare myself," allowed Pat, smoothly covering the young couple's joy. "We can probably manage without wasting Lanark's valuable time—thanks all the same, Colonel."

VanOsdell, Haskins and even Baker, the sober scout, all joined in the chuckle occasioned by the dryness of his tone.

ROOTIN' TOOTIN' READ-EM-UPS FROM ZANE GREY